Five Thousand Miles Underground

Roy Rockwood

Contents

FIVE THOUSAND MILES UNDERGROUND

BY

Roy Rockwood

CHAPTER I
WASHINGTON BACKS OUT

W ASHINGTON! I say Washington!"
Throughout a big shed, filled for the most part with huge pieces of machinery, echoed the voice of Professor Amos Henderson. He did not look up from a small engine over which he was bending.

"Washington! Where are you? Why don't you answer me?"

From somewhere underneath an immense pile of iron, steel and aluminum came the voice of a colored man.

"Yas sir, Perfesser, I'se goin' t' saggasiate my bodily presence in yo' contiguous proximity an' attend t' yo' immediate conglomerated prescriptions at th' predistined period. Yas, sir!"

"Well, Washington, if you had started when you began that long speech you would have been at least half way here by this time. Hurry up! Never mind tightning those bolts now. Find the boys. I need them to help me with this engine. They must be around somewhere."

"I seen 'em goin' fishin' down by th' brook a little while ago," answered the negro, crawling out from under what seemed to be a combined airship and watercraft. "Jack says as how yo' gived him permission t' occupy his indisputatious period of levity in endeavorin' t' extract from th' liquid element some specimens of swimmin' creatures."

"If you mean I said he and Mark could go fishing in the brook, you're right, Washington," replied the professor with a smile. "But you waste a lot of time and breath trying to say it. Why, don't you give up using big words?"

"I reckon I was brought up t' it," replied the colored man grinning from ear to ear. He did not always use big words but when he did they were generally the wrong ones. Sometimes, he spoke quite correctly.

"Well, I suppose you can't help it," resumed Mr. Henderson. "However, never mind that. Find the boys and send them to me."

"With th' least appreciatableness amount of postponement," answered the messenger, and he went out.

Washington White, who in color was just the opposite to his name, a general helper and companion to Professor Henderson, found Mark Sampson and Jack Darrow about a quarter of a mile from the big shed, which was in the center of a wooded island off the coast of Maine. The lads were seated on the bank of a small brook, fishing.

"Perfesser wants yo' immediate," said Washington.

"But we haven't caught a single fish," objected Mark.

"Them's the orders from headquarters," replied the colored man. "Yo' both got t' project yo'selves in th' vicinity of th' machine shop. I reckon th' new fangled contraption that th' perfesser is goin' t' navigate th' air an' sail th' angry seas in, am about done. He want's t' try th' engine."

"Come on then," said Jack. "We probably would not catch any fish, anyhow, Mark."

Accompanied by Washington, the youths, each of whom was about eighteen years old, started toward the big shed.

While they are on their way opportunity may be taken to tell a little about them, as well as about Washington and the professor, and the curious craft on which the scientist was working.

A few years before this story opens Mr. Henderson had invented a wonderful electric airship. He had it about completed when, one day, he and the two boys became unexpectedly acquainted, and, as it developed, friends.

Mark and Jack were orphans. After having rather a hard time knocking about the world trying to make a living, they chanced to meet, and resolved to cast their lots together. They boarded a freight train, and, as told in the first volume of this series, entitled, "Through the Air to the North Pole; or the Wonderful Cruise of the Electric Monarch," the cars were wrecked near where Professor Henderson was building his strange craft.

The boys were cared for by the scientist, and, after their recovery from hurts received in the collision, they accepted his invitation to make the trip through the upper regions in the airship, to search for the north pole. With them went Andy Sudds, an old hunter, and Tom Smith and Bill Jones, two farmers, but who were hired as helpers on the voyage. The party had many adventures on the trip, having battles with savage animals and more savage Esquimaux, and were tossed about in terrible storms. After making some scientific observations, which the professor was much interested in, they started back home.

Having found he could successfully sail in the air, Mr. Henderson resolved to try what it might be like under water.

He moved his machine shop to a lonely spot on the Maine coast, and there, with the help of the boys, Washington, Andy and two machinists constructed a submarine boat, called the Porpoise.

In this the professor resolved to seek the south pole, he having a theory that it was surrounded by an open sea. After much hard work the Porpoise was made ready for the voyage.

What occurred on this great trip is described in the second book of this series, called "Under the Ocean to the South Pole, or the Strange Cruise of the Submarine Wonder." In that is told how once more Tom and Bill, with Andy, the boys and Washington, accompanying Professor Henderson, had many thrilling experiences.

They were caught in the grip of the grass of the terrible Sargasso Sea. Monstrous suckers grasped the boat in their powerful arms, and had to be fought off. They were caught in a sea of boiling water and imprisoned between big fields of ice.

By means of strong diving suits they were able to leave the ship and walk about on the bottom of the sea. They visited a graveyard of sunken ships, saw many strange monsters as well as many beautiful fish in the great depths to which they sunk. Many times they were in dire peril but the resources of the professor, the bravery and daring of the boys, no less than the help Washington and Andy Sudds, the hunter, rendered at times, brought them through.

Those of you who read of their adventures will recall the strange island which they came upon in the Atlantic Ocean, far from the coast of South America.

When they first drew near this island they were almost sucked into the depths of a great whirlpool, caused by water pouring down a big hole that seemed to lead far into the earth. They reversed their ship just in time.

But, on going to another side of the island they were able to approach safely, as at this point the great hole was farther from the shore. Then they landed and investigated.

They found the island was almost circular, and the hole was also round, but not in the center of the land. It was an immense cavity, so wide they could not see across, and as for the depth they could only guess at it. Looking down they could only see rolling masses of vapor and clouds caused by the water which poured down from the ocean with the force of a Niagara.

Gazing down into the big hole Mark suggested it might lead to the centre of the earth, which some scientists claim is hollow. The professor admitted that the cavity looked as though it led to China.

They had no means of investigating further the mystery of the opening and returned to their submarine, completing the voyage to the south pole.

It was now about two years since they had come back from that eventful trip. One of the first things the professor did, after docking the Porpoise, was to shut himself up in his study and begin to draw plans. To the questions of the boys he returned no answer for several days. Then he announced he was working on a craft which could both sail on top of the water and navigate the air.

In time the plans were done, and, in order to keep the work secret, the shop was moved to an island which the professor owned.

Parts of the Monarch and the Porpoise were used in constructing the new craft, so there was no need to get other help than that which the boys, Washington and Bill and Tom could give, since the two latter accepted an offer of the professor to remain and work for him. The boys, of course, would not leave their friend.

The professor realized that he had a more difficult task in his new venture than he had set himself on other occasions. For a ship to be light enough to rise in the air, and, at another time, and with no change, to be strong enough to navigate the ocean, was indeed something to tax Mr. Henderson's ingenuity.

However, in the course of a little over a year the larger part of the work was done. Inside the big shed was the huge affair which, it was hoped, would enable its owner to be master of both air and water.

"Did the professor say anything special?" asked Mark of Washington.

"Nope. I reckon he were too busy problamatin' the exact altitude projected in an inverse direction by th' square root of th' new engine when operated at a million times inside of a few seconds, but he didn't say nothin' t' me. I were busy underneath th' ship, fixin' bolts when he tole me t' find yo'. I wouldn't be s'prised if he had th' thing goin' soon."

"Do you think he'll be generating the new gas to-day?" asked Jack eagerly. "That's the most troublesome part; to get that gas right."

"He didn't say nothin' t' me 'bout it," Washington stated, as he walked along beside the two boys. "He jest seemed anxious like."

"We'd better hurry," advised Mark. "He may be at an important part in his experiments and probably needs us. I hope it will work. He has spent many days on it, and we all have worked hard. It ought to be a success."

"Perfesser allers makes things work," declared Washington stoutly.

"That's a good way to feel about it, anyway," observed Mark. "Well, we'll soon know."

The three hurried to the shed which they could see as they rounded a turn of the path through the wood. They noticed an elderly man approaching with a gun on his shoulder. On one arm he carried a game bag.

"Guess Andy got something for dinner," remarked Jack.

"I hopes so, honey," put in Washington. "I'se got a sort of gone feelin' in my stomach!"

"Any luck, Andy?" called Mark, when he came within hailing distance.

"Fine," replied Andy Sudds. "Rabbits and quail. We'll have a good dinner to-morrow."

While Andy entered the living part of the big shed to put away his gun and game, the boys and Washington kept on to the engine room. They found the professor, with Bill and Tom, busy fitting pipes to the small engine which was set up at one side of the structure.

"Come, boys, I need your aid," remarked Mr. Henderson as they entered. "Take off your coats and pitch in. Tighten up these bolts, Jack. Mark, you mix up those chemicals the way I taught you, and see that the dynamo is in working order for Washington to attend to."

In a little while the shop was a veritable hive of industry, and it resounded to the sound of hammers, wrenches and machinery. In the background was the big ship, which seemed like two immense cigars, one above the other, the lower one the larger.

"Where was you calalatin' t' take this here ship when it gits done, Perfesser?" asked Washington, during a lull in the operations.

"Do you remember that big hole in the island we visited on our trip to the south pole?"

"I suah does," answered the colored man.

"We are going to explore that," went on the scientist. "We are going to make a voyage to the interior of the earth in our Flying Mermaid."

"Go down into th' earth!" exclaimed Washington, his eyes big with fright.

"Certainly; why not?"

"Not for mine!" cried the colored man, dropping the wrench he was holding. "No sire I'm not goin' t' project myself int' a grave while I'se alive. Time enough when I kicks th' bucket. No sir! If yo' an' the boys wants t' risk yo' se'ves goin' down int' th' interior of th' earth, where th' Bible says there's fiery furnaces, yo' kin go, but Washington White stays on terra cotta! That's where he stays; He ain't ready t' be buried, not jest yet!" and the frightened colored man started to leave the shed.

CHAPTER II
THE FLYING MERMAID

HERE! Stop him!" cried Professor Henderson. "Don't let him get away. We still need his help to get the ship in shape. He needn't be frightened. We're not going to start at once."

Mark and Jack ran after Washington, whose progress was somewhat impeded because he kept looking back as if he feared the new ship was chasing him.

"Come on back!" said Mark. "There's no danger, and if there was we're not going to start to-day."

"Ain't yo' foolin' me?" asked Washington, pausing and looking doubtfully at the boys.

"Of course not," answered Mark. "You know Professor Henderson would not make you do anything you didn't want to do, Wash. He wishes you to stay and help him get ready, that's all."

"Well, Washington," observed the aged scientist. "I didn't think you'd go back on me."

"I'd do mos' anything fer yo', Perfesser," said the colored man, "but I got t' beg off this time," and he looked at the Flying Mermaid as if he thought the metal sides would open and devour him.

Then help me get things in shape to generate the gas," the scientist said. "I want to give the new vapor the first real test in lifting power to-day. On the success of it depends the future of the ship."

Seeing there was no immediate danger of being carried to the centre of the earth, Washington resumed his labors. The professor, the boys, Bill and Tom were also hurrying matters to enable a test to be made before night.

As will readily be seen, even by those not familiar with the construction of air-ships and submarines, the chief problem was to find some agent strong enough to lift from the earth a weight heavier than had ever before been put into an apparatus that was destined to traverse the clouds. For the Flying Mermaid was not only an airship but an ocean voyager as well. It had to be made light enough to be lifted far above the earth, yet the very nature of it, necessitating it being made heavy enough to stand the buffeting of the waves and the pressure of water, was against its flying abilities.

Professor Henderson realized this and knew that the chief concern would be to discover a gas or vapor with five times the lifting power of hydrogen, one of the lightest gases known, and one sometimes used to inflate balloons.

After long study he had been partially successful, but he knew from experiments made that the gas he had so far been able to manufacture would not answer. What he wanted was some element that could be mixed with the gas, to neutralize the attraction of gravitation, or downward pull of the earth.

While he was seeking this, and experimenting on many lines, the construction of the air-water ship went on. In general the outward construction was two cigar shaped hulls, one above the other. Aluminum, being the lightest and strongest metal that could be used for the purpose, formed the main part of both bodies.

The upper hull was one hundred feet long and twenty feet in diameter at the widest part. It tapered to points at either end. It was attached to the lower hull by strong braces, at either end, while from the center there extended a pipe which connected with the lower section. This pipe was intended to convey the lifting gas to the part which corresponded to the bag of the balloon, save that it was of metal instead of silk, or rubber as is usual.

There were two reasons for this. One was that it would not be liable to puncture, particularly in the proposed underground trip, and the other was that it did not have to be so large as a cloth bag would have had to be. It was also a permanent part of the ship, and on a voyage where part of the time the travelers would be in the air and part on the water, and when the change from one to the other would have to be made quickly, this was necessary. It would have taken too long to raise the ship in the air had a cloth bag been used to contain the gas.

The lower hull or main part of the craft was one hundred and fifty feet long, and forty feet through at the largest part, in the centre.

It was divided into four sections. The forward one contained the sleeping quarters of Professor Henderson and his crew. There was a small stateroom for each one. Above was a conning or observation tower, reached by a small flight of steps. From this tower the ship could be steered, stopped and started, as could also be done from the engine room, which was in the after part of the hull.

As in the Porpoise and Monarch, electricity formed the motive power and was also used for many other purposes on board. Engines operated by gas produced the current which heated, lighted and moved the ship, as well as played a part in producing the wonderful gas.

The ship moved forward or backward by means of a novel arrangement. This was by the power of compressed air. From either end of the lower hull there projected a short pipe working in a ball and socket joint, so it could be turned in any direction. By means of strong pumps a current of compressed air could be sent out from either pipe. Thus when floating above the earth the ship was forced forward by the blast of air rushing from the pipe at the stern. It was the same principle as that on which a sky rocket is shot heavenward, save that gases produced by the burning of powder in the pasteboard rocket form its moving impulse.

In the case of the Flying Mermaid, it could be made to move backward by sending the air out of the forward tube. Thus, when in the water, the compressed air rushing from the pipe struck the fluid and forced the ship forward or backward as was desired. It floated on the surface, the deck being about three feet out of water, while the aluminum gas bag was overhead.

The engine room was a marvel of machine construction. It contained pumps for air and water, motors, dynamos, gas engines, and a maze of wheels and levers. Yet everything was very compact and no room was wasted.

The use of the air method of propulsion did away with the necessity of a large propellor such as most airships have to use, a propellor which must of necessity be very light and which is easily broken.

Next to the engine room was the kitchen. It contained an electric range and all necessary appliances and utensils for preparing meals. There were lockers and a large reserve storeroom which when the time came would be well stocked with food. Forward of the kitchen was the living and dining room. It contained comfortable seats, folding tables and a small library. Here, also were many instruments designed to show how the various machines were working. There were gages, pointers and dials, which told the direction the ship was traveling, the speed and the distance above the earth or below the surface. Similar indicators were in the conning tower, which had a powerful search light.

The ship was lighted throughout by incandescent lamps, and there was even a small automatic piano worked by the electric current, on which popular airs could be played.

If the gas and the gravity neutralizer worked as Professor Henderson hoped they would, as soon as the ship was completed, all that would be necessary to start on the voyage would be to fill the aluminum bag and set the air compressor in motion.

The gas was made from common air, chemically treated and with a secret material added which by means of a complicated machine in a measure did away with the downward pull of the earth. Thus all that was necessary to carry on a long voyage was a quantity of gasolene to operate the engine which worked the electric machines, and some of this secret compound.

The professor and his helpers had been working to good advantage. At last all was in readiness for the gas test.

It was proposed to try it on an experimental scale. Some of the fluid was to be generated and forced into an aluminum cylinder under the same pressure it would be used in the air ship. To this cylinder were attached weights in proportion to the weight of the Flying Mermaid with its load of human freight, engines and equipment.

"This cylinder is just one one-hundredth the size of the cylinder of the ship," said the professor. "I am going to fasten to it a hundred pound weight. If it lifts that our latest contrivance will be a success."

"You mean if the little cylinder pulls a hundred pounds up the big ship will take us and the machinery up?" asked Mark.

"Certainly," answered the professor. "If this cylinder lifts a hundred pounds, one a hundred times as big (as that of the Mermaid is), will lift a hundred times as much, or ten thousand pounds. That is five tons, or more than a ton over what I figure to be the weight of our ship and contents. The latest war balloon can lift one ton with ease, and if my machine can not do five times as well I shall be disappointed."

The last adjustments were made, pipes were run from the gas generator to the cylinder, and the hundred pound weight was attached.

"Everybody look out now," said Mr. Henderson. "I am going to start the machine and let the gas enter the cylinder. It is a very powerful gas and may break the cylinder. If it does you must all duck."

The scientist gave a last look at everything. The boys got behind some boards whence they could see without being in danger. Washington, who had little fear so long as there was no danger of going under ground, took his place at the dynamo. Andy Sudds, with Bill and Tom, stationed themselves in safe places.

"All ready!" called the professor.

He pulled a lever toward him, turned a wheel and signalled to Washington to start the dynamo. There was a sound of buzzing machinery, which was followed by a hiss as the gas began to enter the cylinder under pressure. Would it stand the strain? That question was uppermost in every one's mind save the professor's. He only cared to see the cylinder leave the ground, carrying the weight with it. That would prove his long labors were crowned with success.

Faster and faster whirred the dynamo. The gas was being generated from the air. The secret chemical made a hissing which could be heard for some distance. The gage registered a heavy pressure. Anxiously the professor watched the cylinder.

"There!" he exclaimed at length. "It has all the gas it can hold. Now to see if it works!"

He disconnected the pipe leading from the generator. This left the cylinder free. It seemed to tremble slightly. There appeared to be a movement to the hundred pound weight which rested on the ground. It was as if it was tugging to get loose.

"There it goes! There it goes!" cried Mark, joyfully.

"Hurrah!" shouted Jack. "There she rises!"

"It suttinly am projectin' itself skyward!" yelled Washington, coming from the dynamo.

Sure enough the cylinder was slowly rising in the air, bearing the weight with it. It had lifted it clear from the ground and was approaching the roof of the big shed.

"It will work! It will work!" exclaimed the professor, strangely excited.

The next instant the cylinder, carrying the weight, sailed right out of an open skylight, and began drifting outside the shop, and across the fields.

"Quick! We must get it back!" cried Mr. Henderson. "If it gets away my secret may be discovered and I will lose all! We must secure it!"

But the cylinder was now two hundred feet in the air and being blown to the east, the weight dangling below it, making it look like a miniature airship.

"We can never catch that!" cried Mark.

CHAPTER III
WASHINGTON DECIDES

WE must catch that cylinder!" the professor exclaimed. "Some one may find it when it comes down and analyze the gas. Then he would discover how to make it. The cylinder must come down!"

"Don't see how we can proximate ourselves inter th' vicinity of it lessen we delegate th' imperial functions of orinthological specimens t' some member of this here party," observed Washington.

"If you mean we can't catch that there contraption unless we turn into birds I'll show you that you're mistaken!" cried Andy Sudds. "I guess I have a trick or two up my sleeve," and the old hunter quickly threw open the breech of his gun and inserted a couple of cartridges.

He raised the piece to his shoulder and took quick aim. There was a sliver of flame, a puff of smoke and a sharp report. The professor and the boys who were watching the cylinder saw it vibrate up in the air. Then there came a whistling sound. An instant later the metal body began to descend, and it and the weight fell to the earth.

"I'm sorry I had to put a bullet through it, Professor," said old Andy with a queer smile, "but it was the only way I saw of bringing it down. Hope it isn't damaged much."

"It doesn't matter if it is," the scientist answered. "I can make more cylinders, but I don't want that secret of the gas to become known. Your bullet served a good turn, Andy, for it let the compressed vapor out just in time."

"Then we may consider the experiment a success," said Mark, as Washington went to where the cylinder had fallen, to detach it from the weight and bring both to the shed.

"It seems so," Mr. Henderson answered. "True, it was only an experiment. We have yet to test the ship itself."

"When can we do that?" asked Jack.

"I hope by Monday," the scientist answered.

"Will you try it in the water or air first?" asked Mark.

"I'm almost certain it will float in the water," the aged inventor said. "It does not require much work to make a ship which will do that. But the air proposition is another matter. However, since the cylinder rose, I am pretty sure the Flying Mermaid will.

"But we have done enough work to-day. Let's rest and have something to eat. Then, with Sunday to sit around and talk matters over, we will be ready for Monday's test."

Some of the game Andy had killed was soon on the table, for Washington, in addition to his other accomplishments, was an expert cook. During the evening the boys and their friends sat in the living room of the big shed and talked over the events of the day.

Sunday was spent in discussing what adventures might lie before them should they be able to descend into the big hole. Washington did not say, much, but it was easy to see he had no notion of going. He even began to pack his few belongings in readiness to leave the service of Mr. Henderson, for whom he had worked a good many years.

No one remained long abed Monday morning. Even Washington was up early in spite of the interest he had lost in the professor's voyage.

"I jest wants t' see yo' start fer that place where they buries live folks," he said.

In order to properly test the Flying Mermaid it was necessary to move the craft from the shed from which place it had never been taken since it's construction was started. It had been built on big rollers in anticipation of this need, so that all which was now necessary was to open the doors at the end, and roll the craft out. This was accomplished with no small amount of labor, and it was nearly noon before the big ship was moved into the open. It was shoved along to a little clearing in front of the shed, where no trees would interfere with its possible upward movement.

Everyone was bustling about. The professor was busiest of all. He went from one machine to another; from this apparatus to that, testing here, turning wheels there, adjusting valves and seeing that all was in readiness for the generating of the powerful gas.

As the airship was half round on the bottom and as it rested in a sort of semi-circular cradle; it brought the entrance some distance above the ground. To make it easier to get in and out while preparations for the trial were going on, Bill and Tom had made an improvised pair of steps, which were tied to the side of the ship with ropes.

Up and down these the professor, the boys and Andy went, taking in tools and materials, and removing considerable refuse which had accumulated during the building of the craft.

Finally all was in readiness for starting the making of the gas. The ship was not wholly complete and no supplies or provisions for the long voyage had been taken aboard. The Flying Mermaid was about a ton lighter than it would be when fully fitted out, but to make up for this the professor had left in the ship a lot of tools and surplus machinery so that the craft held as much weight as it would under normal conditions. If the gas lifted it now it would at any other time.

"Start the generator," said Mr. Henderson, to Mark. "We'll soon see whether we are going to succeed or fail."

The boy turned a number of levers and wheels. The machine which made the powerful vapor was soon in operation. The professor had already added enough of the secret compound to the tank containing the other ingredients, and the big pump was sucking in air to be transformed into the lifting gas.

The boys and the professor were in the engine room. Andy Sudds, with Bill and Tom, had taken their places in the living room, to more evenly balance the ship, since the things in it were not yet all in their proper places. As for Washington he was busy running from the shed to the ship with various tools and bits of machinery the professor desired.

The gas was being generated rapidly. Throughout the ship there resounded a hissing noise that told it was being forced through the pipe into the aluminum shell above the ship proper.

"I wonder how soon it will begin to lift us," said Mark.

"It will take about half an hour," replied Mr. Henderson. "You see we have first to fill the holder completely, since there is no gas in it. After this we will keep some on hand, so that it will only need the addition of a small quantity to enable the ship to rise."

He was busy watching the pointer on a dial which indicated the pressure of the gas, and the lifting force. The boys were kept busy making adjustments to the machinery and oiling bearings.

Suddenly, throughout the length of the craft there was felt a curious trembling. It was as though the screw of a powerful steamer was revolving in the water.

"What is it?" asked Jack.

"I hope it is the lifting power of the gas making itself felt," the professor answered. "Perhaps the Flying Mermaid is getting ready to try her wings."

The trembling became more pronounced. The gas was being generated faster than ever. The whole ship was trembling. Tom and Bill came from the room, where they were stationed, to inquire the meaning, but were reassured by the professor.

"Don't be alarmed if you find yourselves up in the air pretty soon," he remarked with a smile. "Remember the Electric Monarch, and the flights she took. We may not go as high as we did in her, but it will answer the same purpose."

The gas was hissing through the big tube as it rushed into the overhead holder. The gage indicated a heavy pressure. The ship began to tremble more violently and to sway slightly from side to side.

"I think we shall rise presently," said Mr. Henderson. His voice showed the pride he felt at the seeming success with which his invention was about to meet.

Suddenly, with a little jerk, as though some one with a giant hand had plucked the Flying Mermaid from the earth, the ship gave a little bound into the air, and was floating free.

"Here we go!" cried Mr. Henderson. "The ship is a success. Now we're off for the hole in the earth!"

The Flying Mermaid was indeed rising in the air. True it did not go up so swiftly as had the Monarch, but then it was a much heavier and stronger vessel, and flying was only one of its accomplishments.

"It's a success! It's a success!" shouted Mark, capering about in his excitement.

"Now we'll see what the centre of the earth looks like," went on Jack. "I can hardly wait for the time to come when we are to start on the voyage."

At that instant, when the ship was but a few feet from the ground, but slowly rising, the boys and the professor heard a shouting below them.

"What's that?" asked the scientist. "Is any one hurt?"

Mark ran to a small window, something like a port hole in an ocean steamer, and looked out.

"Quick!" he shouted. "Stop the ship! Washington will be killed!"

In fact from the agonized yells which proceeded from somewhere under the craft it seemed that the accident was in process of happening.

"Save me! Save me!" cried the colored man. "I'm goin' to fall! Catch me, some one!"

"What is it?" asked the professor, making ready to shut off the power and let the ship settle back to earth, from which it had moved about fifty feet.

"It's Washington," explained Mark. "He evidently tried to walk up the steps just as the boat mounted skyward. He rolled down and managed to grab the end of the rope which was left over after the steps were tied. Now he's swinging down there."

"Are you going to lower the ship?" asked Jack.

"Of course!" exclaimed the professor. "I only hope he hangs on until his feet touch the earth."

"Keep a tight hold!" shouted Mark, from out of the small window.

"That's th' truest thing yo' ever said!" exclaimed Washington. "You bet I'm goin' to hold on, and I'm comin' up too," which he proceeded to do, hand over hand, like a sailor.

The boys and the professor watched the colored man's upward progress. The ship had hardly begun to settle as, in the excitement, not enough gas had been let out. Closer and closer came Washington, until he was able to grasp the edge of the opening, to which the steps were fastened.

"I thought you weren't coming with us," observed the professor, when he saw that his helper was safe.

"I changed my mind," said the colored man. "It's jest luck. Seems like th' ship done wanted me t' go 'long, an' I'm goin'. I'll take my chances on bein' buried alive. I ain't never seen th' centre of th' earth, an' I want's to 'fore I die. I'm goin' 'long, Perfessor!"

CHAPTER IV
WHAT DID MARK SEE?

WELL, I'm glad you've decided at last," the professor remarked. "Now come inside and we'll see how the ship works."

Once over his fright, Washington made himself at home on the craft he had helped build. He went from one room to another and observed the engine.

"She certainly am workin'" he observed with pride. "Are we still goin' up, Perfessor?"

"Still mounting," replied Mr. Henderson, "We are now three hundred feet above the earth," he added as he glanced at a registering gage.

The great air pump was set going and soon from the after tube, a big stream of the compressed vapor rushed. It acted on the ship instantly and sent the craft ahead at a rapid rate. By elevating or depressing the tube the craft could be sent obliquely up or down. Then, by forcing the air from the forward tube, the Mermaid was reversed and scudded backward.

But it was more with the ship's ability to rise and descend that Professor Henderson was concerned, since on that depended their safety. So various tests were made, in generating the gas and using the negative gravity apparatus.

All worked to perfection. Obeying the slightest turn of the wheels and levers the Mermaid rose or fell. She stood still, suspended herself in the air, or rushed backward and forward.

Of course the machinery was new and did not operate as smoothly as it would later, but the professor and his friends were very well satisfied.

"Now we'll try something new," said the scientist to the two boys as they stood beside him in the tower. "I only hope this part succeeds, and we shall soon be off on our voyage."

He turned several levers. There was a hissing sound as the gas rushed from the container, and the ship began to settle down.

"What's th' matter? Are we goin' t' hit th' earth?" yelled Washington, rushing from the engine room.

"Keep quiet," ordered the professor. "We are only going down, that's all."

"But good land! Perfesser!" exclaimed the colored man. "The ocean's right under us! You forgot you sailed sway from the island! We'll be drowned suah!"

"Leave it to me," said Mr. Henderson. "The Flying Mermaid is going to take a bath!"

"As long as it swims it will be all right," observed Mark in a low tone to Jack. "I'm glad I can take care of myself in the water."

Before Jack could reply the Mermaid seemed to take a sudden dive through the air. The next instant she struck the water with a splash that sent the waves rolling all about. The craft rocked violently to and fro on the surface of the sea. For a while there were anxious hearts aboard, for there was no certainty but that the ship might not sink to the bottom.

But the old professor had not calculated and builded in vain. After rocking about like a vessel newly launched, the strange craft rode safely and upright on the water. It set down far enough to bring the propelling tubes well under, but not so far but that the conning tower was well out and there was a small deck available.

"Now to see if we can conquer the water as we did the air!" cried the professor. "Mark, start the air pump. Jack, you steer, for I want to watch the machinery under the additional strain."

From the rear tube rushed such a volume of air that the ocean near it bubbled and foamed. The ship trembled from stem to stern, and then, after hanging for an instant as if undecided what to do, it began to move forward as easily as though it had never sailed any other element than the sea.

"She fits her name!" the professor cried. "She is indeed the Flying Mermaid, for she sails the ocean as easily as she navigates in the clouds!"

For a mile or two the craft was sent ahead over the waves. Then it was reversed and run backwards. Satisfied that his long months of work had not gone for naught, the professor after trying several experiments, decided to try and raise the ship while in motion.

With Jack and Mark to look after the air pumps, while Washington, Tom and Bill busied themselves in the engine room, Mr. Henderson began to generate the gas and start the negative gravity apparatus. All the while the craft was forging ahead.

There was again the hissing sound that told of the aluminum holder being filled. For a few minutes there seemed to be no change, the Mermaid plowing forward.

Then like a bird rising from the waves, or like a flying fish leaping from the sea to escape some pursuing monster of the deep, the new ship shot up diagonally from the surface and winged its way into the upper regions of the air.

"Success! Success!" cried the professor. "This proves all I wanted to know. Now. we are ready for our great trip!"

Great were the rejoicings in the camp that night. It was like living over again the days when they were aboard the diving Porpoise or the flying Monarch. To the recollections were added the anticipations of what was before them in the trip to the interior of the earth.

Busy days followed, for there was still much to be done to the Flying Mermaid. The machinery, which was only partly completed, had to be finished. Besides this the professor was working on some apparatus, the use of which he did not disclose to any one. It was stored aboard the ship at the last minute.

Plenty of provisions had to be taken aboard, and many supplies needed to work the Mermaid and insure that it would go to the end of the voyage. The materials for generating the gas and negative gravity, spare parts, records for the automatic piano and other things were stored away.

Some guns and ammunition were taken along as were a few revolvers, since old Andy had said it was best to prepare for any thing in the shape of enemies or wild beasts that might be met with in the interior regions.

It was decided to make the start by sailing along the surface of the sea for several days, as in the event of any weakness in the machinery being discovered there would be less danger. If, at the end of four days, no trouble developed, the professor said he would send the Mermaid into the air and make the rest of the voyage through the sky.

The night before the start was to be made the professor, with the boys, Washington and the other helpers, went about through the various shops and buildings, locking them up securely. For they could not tell how long they would be away, and they had to leave behind much valuable material.

As there were several things that needed attention they divided the work up. Mark had finished his share and was walking back toward the living cabin where they were all quartered, when, down at the shore, near where the boat was moored, he fancied he saw, in the gathering darkness, a moving figure.

"I wonder who that can be," he thought. "All the others are near the machine shop, for I just left them there. Perhaps it's some one trying to spy out how the Mermaid is built."

Knowing the professor wanted his secret well guarded, Mark walked softly toward the little dock that served as a place whence the Mermaid could be easily boarded. As he approached he saw the figure moving. Something struck the boy as peculiar.

Though the object had some of the characteristics of a man it did not walk like a human being, but shuffled along more like a huge ape or monkey. It seemed bent over, as if it stooped toward the ground.

"Who are you?" called Mark suddenly.

For an instant the figure halted and then hurried on faster than before, with a curious, shuffling walk. It was approaching the ship.

Somehow it struck Mark as if it was an uncanny being; an inhabitant of some other world. Then he laughed at his half-fear, and started on a run toward the dock.

"If it's some tramp trying to find a place to sleep he'd better not go aboard the ship, he might do some damage," the boy thought.

He could hardly see the figure now as it had passed into the shadow cast by the boat. He was about to summon the professor to make an investigation, when Washington started going the search light which was placed just over the door of the living cabin. It was kept there as a sort of beacon light, as, near the island was a dangerous ledge of rocks.

Then, in the blinding white glare from the big lantern as Washington accidentally swung it toward the Mermaid, Mark beheld a strange sight.

The figure he had been watching stood out in bold relief. Though it was shaped like a human being it was not like any person the boy had ever seen. It seemed covered with a skin twice too large for it; a skin, which, in spite of the clothes that concealed it, hung in folds about the arms and legs, dropping pendent like from the neck like a big garment, and flapping in the wind.

For an instant Mark was so startled he cried out, and the professor and the others ran to see what was the matter.

"There-- by the ship! A horrible creature!" exclaimed Mark.

Shouting to Washington to keep the light steady in the direction of the dock, Mr. Henderson ran toward the moored Mermaid. Jack, Andy, Bill and Tom, with Mark in the rear followed him.

"Nothing here," said the scientist, after a careful search about. "Are you sure you saw something, Mark?"

"Positively," replied the lad with a shudder. He described the vision of the darkness.

"I guess it was a big otter, or maybe an enormous turtle," the professor said.

CHAPTER V
ATTACKED BY A WHALE

BUT Mark was certain it was nothing like that, though a careful search failed to reveal anything or any person near the ship. It was too dark to examine for footprints, and even Mark, after taking a look all about, felt he might have been deceived by shadows. Still he was a little nervous, and could hardly sleep for imagining what the thing he saw could have been.

The next day every one was so busy that no one, not even Mark, recalled the little excitement of the night before. Shortly after noon, final preparations having been made, they all got aboard the Mermaid and started off.

It was a bright sunshiny day, and the craft, speeding away from the island where it had been constructed, over the dancing blue waves, must have presented a strange sight had there been any spectators. For surely no such ship had ever before sailed those waters.

However, there was no other vessel in sight, and the island, as far as the professor and his friends knew, had never been inhabited.

"We will not try for any great speed," Mr. Henderson remarked as he, with Mark and Jack, stood in the conning tower managing the Mermaid. "We don't want to strain any joints at the start or heat any engine bearings. There will be time enough for speed later."

"Yes, and we may need it more when we get into the centre of the earth than we do now," observed Mark.

"Why so?" asked Jack.

"No telling what we may run up against underneath the ground," went on Mark. "We may have to fight strange animals and stranger beings. Besides, the atmosphere and water there can't be the same as up here; do you think so, Professor?"

For a few minutes the scientist was silent. He seemed to be thinking deeply.

"I will tell you what I believe," he said at length. "I have never spoken of it before, but now that we are fairly started and may eventually have a chance to prove my theory, I will say that I think the centre of this earth on which we live is hollow. Inside of it, forming a core, so to speak, I believe there is another earth, similar to ours in some respects which revolves inside this larger sphere."

They were well out to sea now, as they could observe when they emerged on the little deck. Above their heads was the aluminum gas holder, which served as a sort of protection from the sun that was quite warm. The Mermaid rode with an easy motion, being submerged just enough to make her steady, yet not deep enough to encounter much resistance from the water. In fact it could not have been arranged better for speed or comfort.

"I think we will sail well to the eastward before making our course south," Mr. Henderson said. "I do not care to meet too many ships, as those aboard will be very curious and I do not want too much news of this venture to get out. We will take an unfrequented route and avoid delays by being hailed by every passing vessel whose captain will wonder what queer craft he had met with."

The boys enjoyed the sail, for the weather could not have been better. Even old Andy, who seldom said much, seemed delighted with the prospect of having strange adventures. He had his rifle with him, and, indeed, he seldom went anywhere that he did not carry it.

"For there's no telling when you may see something you want to shoot or that ought to be shot," he used to say, "and it's always the man without a gun who needs it most. So I'm taking no chances."

They sailed all that afternoon without meeting with a craft of any kind. Straight to the east they went, and when night began to settle down Washington got supper. It was decided to run slowly after dark until all hands were more familiar with the ship.

Morning found the Mermaid about a hundred miles from the island where she had been launched. The night had been uneventful, except that Mark told Jack he heard some strange noise near his bunk several times. He was nearest the storeroom where spare parts, and the curious cylinder the professor had brought aboard, were kept.

"I guess it was rats," said Jack. "They are always in ships."

"Old wooden ships, yes," admitted Mark. "But I'll bet there's not a rat aboard the Mermaid."

"Then you were dreaming," said Jack, as if that settled it.

Mark did not speak further of the noise, but he did considerable thinking. However, the next night there was no further disturbance.

The fourth day out, when everything had passed off well, the engines doing their best, the professor decided to speed them up a bit, since he was satisfied they had "found" themselves as mechanics term it.

"We'll see how fast we can go through the water," said Mr. Henderson, "and then I think we can safely turn our course south. We are well beyond the ordinary lines of travel now."

Having oiled the bearings well, and seen that everything was in place and properly adjusted, the professor and the boys took their places in the conning tower, while Washington, Tom and Bill remained in the engine room. Andy stayed on deck with his gun.

"I might see a big fish, and we could vary our bill of fare," he said with a laugh.

"Here we go!" exclaimed the professor as he shifted the levers and turned some wheels and valves. "Now we'll see how fast we can travel."

As he spoke the Mermaid responded to the added impulse of the compressed air and shot through the water at a terrific speed. The sudden increase in momentum almost threw the boys from their feet, and they would have fallen had they not grasped some projecting levers.

"I guess that will do," Said the scientist. "I think we have speed enough for almost any emergency. I'll let her run at this rate for a while, and then we'll slack up."

Looking ahead, the boys could see the green waters parting in front of the bow of the Mermaid, as if to make room for her. Two huge waves were thrown upon either side.

Suddenly, dead ahead, there loomed up a big black object.

"Look out you'll hit the rock!" cried Mark to the professor, who was steering.

With a turn of his wrist Mr. Henderson moved the wheel which controlled the tube. It was deflected and sent the boat to larboard.

At that instant from the rock two small fountains of water rose in the air, falling back in a shower of spray through which the sun gleamed.

"That's not a rock! It's a big whale!" cried Jack. "And we're going to hit him!"

The professor had miscalculated the speed of the craft, or else had not thrown her far enough to larboard, for, a second later, the Mermaid was almost upon the big leviathan.

With a desperate twirling of the steering wheel the professor veered the craft as far as possible. But all he could do did not suffice, for the craft hit the whale a glancing blow on the side, and the ship careened as if she would turn turtle.

At the same time there rang out from upon deck the sound of a rifle shot. Old Andy had taken a chance at the enormous creature of the deep.

"Hurrah!" the bays heard him shout. "I give him one plumb in the eye! A fine shot! And we hit him besides with the boat. I guess he's a goner!"

"I'm afraid not," muttered the professor. "That was a bad blow we struck him, but I think it will only ruffle his temper. We'll have to look sharp now, boys."

By this time the ship had rushed past the whale, but the boys, looking through a window in the rear of the tower could see the huge body. Now the fountains of water which the whale spouted were tinged with red.

"He's bleeding!" exclaimed the professor. "I guess Andy hit him in a vital spot."

"But not vital enough!" cried Mark. "See! He's coming after us!"

And so it proved. The whale, angered, and, probably half crazed by the pain of the bullet and the blow, was coursing after the ship, coming on with the speed of an express train. Straight at the Mermaid he lunged his huge bulk.

"We must escape him!" cried Mr. Henderson. "If he hits us he'll send us to the bottom!"

He had made ready to slow up the Mermaid to see if it had sustained any damage from the impact with the whale, but when he saw the monster coming after the boat he knew the only safety lay in flight.

"Let us go up into the air and so escape him!" cried Jack, with sudden inspiration.

For an instant neither Mark nor the professor grasped what Jack meant. Then, with an exclamation, the professor pulled forward the lever that generated the gas and set working the gravity neutralizer, which would enable the ship to rise.

Faster through the water went the Mermaid, and faster after her came the whale. Above the hum of the engines was heard the hiss of the powerful gas. The ship trembled more violently.

"We are rising!" exclaimed the professor, as he looked at a gage.

The boys could feel the craft lifting from the waves which clung to her as if they hated to lose her. The boys knew the gas was beginning to operate.

"If it is not too late!" whispered Mark, half to himself.

For the monster of the seas was coming on, lashing the water to foam with his terrible flukes, and sending aloft a bloody spray. His speed was awful.

Now he was but ten feet away from the fleeing craft-- now but eight-- now five! Ten seconds more and the big head, like the blunt stern of a battle ship, forced forward by the tons of blubber, flesh, bone and fat behind it would strike the Mermaid and crush it like an egg shell.

Now if ever was the need for the Flying Mermaid to prove herself worthy of the name. Now, if ever, was the time for her to leave the watery element and take to the lighter one.

And she did. With a last tremble, as if to free herself from the hold of the waves, the gallant craft soared up into the air, leaving the water, which dripped from her keel like a fountain's spray, and shooting aloft like a bird, escaped her terrible enemy which passed under her, so close that the lower part of the Flying Mermaid scraped the whale's back.

"Saved!" exclaimed the professor.

CHAPTER VI
THE CYCLONE

IT was only in the nick of time, for a second later and the big mammal of the ocean would have struck the ship and split it from stem to stern.

Higher and higher into the air mounted the Flying Mermaid, while in the water below, the whale, incensed by missing his prey, was lashing the waves to foam.

"Well, that was a narrow squeak; as close as I ever care to come to it!" exclaimed Andy as he let go of the steel rail to which he was clinging and entered the conning tower. "I had no idea of hitting the big fish."

"I guess he would have taken after us whether you had fired at him or not," said Mr. Henderson. "He was probably looking for trouble, and took the first thing that came in his way, which happened to be us. Some whales are like that, so I have read; big bull creatures, exiled from the school to which they once belonged, they get like mad creatures and know neither friend nor foe. Something like rogue elephants, I imagine."

Now, having thus unexpectedly risen into the air, the professor decided to continue travel in that style for a while at least. It would require less force to propel the ship, and the going would be more comfortable, since in the upper regions the Mermaid rode on an even keel, while in the water there was more or less rolling, due to the action of the waves.

Once recovered from their fright caused by the whale, and having lost sight of the enormous creature, for they were now far above the ocean, the adventurers began to think of something to eat.

Washington lost little time in preparing a meal, and it was eaten with a relish. The electric cooking stove worked to perfection, for the colored man had learned how to use that aboard the Porpoise and Monarch, and could be depended on to turn out appetizing dishes.

"What do you say to traveling through the air at night?" asked Mr. Henderson, as he arose from the table.

"Suits me," replied Mark. "There's less danger than in the water, I think,"

Bill, Tom and Washington arranged to stand the night watch, and, when the professor had examined the engines and given orders about keeping the ship on her course through the air, he retired to his bunk. Jack and Mark soon followed.

It must have been about midnight when Mark was awakened by a movement that seemed to come from the storeroom next to where his sleeping place was located. At first he thought he had been dreaming, but, as he found he was wide awake, he knew it was no imagination that had affected him.

"I certainly heard something," he said to himself. "It sounded just as it did the other night. I wonder if I ought to investigate."

He thought over the matter carefully as he sat upright in his bunk in the darkness. True the noise might be a natural one, due to the vibration of the engine, or to some echo from the machinery. As Mark listened he heard it again.

This time he realized it was the slow movement of some heavy body. He felt a cold shiver run over him and his hair evinced an uncomfortable tendency to stand upright. But he conquered his feelings and resolved to keep cool and see if he could discover what had awakened him.

He got up and moved softly about the little room that contained his bunk. He could hear better now, and knew it was no echo or vibration that had come to his ears.

Once again he heard the strange sound. It was exactly the same as before; as if some big creature was pulling itself over the floor.

"Maybe it's a snake; a water snake!" thought Mark. "It may have crawled aboard when we did not notice it."

Then he remembered that the ship had not been open in any way that would enable a serpent to come on it, since it had been started on its ocean trip. Before that, he was sure no snake had entered the Flying Mermaid. Still it sounded more like a snake than anything else.

"I'm going to make a search," decided the boy.

He took a small portable electric light, run by a storage battery, and, slipping on a pair of shoes and a bath robe, he left his stateroom.

He had decided that the noise came from the storage compartment and so made for that. The door he knew was not locked, since he had seen Mr. Henderson go in late that afternoon, and the professor had used no key.

Moving softly, Mark left his room and soon found himself in a corridor, on either side of which were located the sleeping quarters of the others. He did not want to awaken them, and, perhaps, be laughed at for his curiosity.

To get to the storeroom Mark had to go first from the corridor into the dining room. He soon reached the door that guarded what he thought might be a strange secret. Trying the knob softly he found it giving under his fingers.

"I wonder if I had better go in," he thought. "Perhaps, after all, it was only rats, as Jack said."

But, even as he listened he again heard the odd sound coming from the room. This determined him. He would solve the mystery if possible.

Cautiously he turned the knob. The door was slowly swinging open when Mark was startled by a noise from behind him. He turned suddenly to see Professor Henderson confronting him.

"What is it, Mark? Is the ship on fire? What's the matter? Is any one hurt?"

"I was just going in this room to----" began Mark.

"Don't do it! Don't do it!" exclaimed the professor in an excited whisper. "No one must go in that room. I forgot to tell you and Jack about it. No one must enter. It contains a secret!"

"I heard a strange noise and----" Mark began again.

"It could make no noise! It would be impossible for it to make a noise!" the professor exclaimed.

"I heard something," the boy insisted.

"You were dreaming!" said the professor. "Now go back to bed, Mark, and don't let this happen again. Remember, no one must enter that room unless I give permission!"

Somewhat crestfallen at the outcome of his investigations, but realizing that the professor could do what he wanted to aboard his own ship, Mark went back to bed. But he could not sleep. All the rest of the night he was wondering whether Mr.

Henderson had some strange creature hidden aboard the Mermaid. He feared lest the old scientist's mind might be affected and, in his wildness he had made some infernal machine that would, in time, blow the whole ship apart.

But tired nature asserted itself at last, and, weary with vain imaginings, Mark fell into a slumber. The next morning he awoke with a start from a dream that he was being devoured by an immense water snake.

He said nothing to the others about his night's adventure, for, as it transpired, no one else had been awakened by his investigations. The professor did not refer to his conversation with Mark.

"There's something queer going on aboard the ship this trip," said Mark to himself. "But I guess it's none of my business. Professor Henderson seems to know what he is doing and I guess I can trust him."

He resolved to think no more of the strange noises and movements, and, for several nights thereafter he was not disturbed by them.

The weather, which, up to this time had been fair, took a sudden turn for the worse about the fourth day after Mark's little night expedition. One evening the sun sank in a mass of dull lead-colored clouds and a sharp wind sprang up.

"We're going to have a storm," said Mr. Henderson. "It's liable to be a bad one, too, from the way the barometer is falling."

He looked at the glass, and scanned the various instruments that told how high up the Mermaid was and how fast she was traveling.

"We're pretty high up in the air," he said, "and scooting along at about fifty miles an hour. We are going against the wind, too, but fortunately it is not blowing hard."

At that moment there sounded from without a peculiar howling sound, as if a siren whistle was being blown.

"'Pears like there's goin' t' be a tumultuous demonstration of sub-maxiliary contortions in th' empherial regions contiguous t' th' upper atmosphere!" exclaimed Washington, entering from the engine room into the conning tower.

"What's the trouble?" asked Mr. Henderson.

"Terrible big black cloud chasin' us from behind!" exclaimed the colored man.

Noting the alarm in Washington's voice the professor glanced from the rear window. What he saw caused him to exclaim:

"It's a cyclone! We must drop down to avoid it!"

He sprang to a lever controlling the gas and yanked it toward him. There was a shrill hissing sound, and a second later the Mermaid began to sink. The boys watching the gages on the wall of the tower, saw that the craft was falling rapidly.

But, with a rush and roar, the terrible wind was upon them. It caught the craft in its fearful grip and heeled it over as a ship careens to the ocean blast.

"It's a storm in the upper regions! We'll find it calm below!" cried the professor above the howling of the gale. He opened the gas outlet wider and the ship fell more rapidly.

"Are you sure we're over the ocean?" asked Mark.

"Positive!" the professor called back. "We have been traveling straight south over the Atlantic for the last week. We will land in the midst of the waters and float safely."

Lower and lower went the Mermaid. The wind was now blowing with the force of a tornado, and, as the craft had to slant in order to descend, it felt the power of the gale more than if it had scudded before it. But, by skilful use of the directing tube, the professor was able to keep the boat from turning over. As they came further down toward the earth the force of the wind was felt less and less, until, as they came within two hundred feet of the water which they saw below them in the gathering dusk, it died out altogether.

"Now we are free from it," said the professor as the Mermaid came down on the waves like an immense swan.

"Are you going ahead or going to stop here?" asked Mark

"We'll keep right on," Mr. Henderson answered. "No telling when the storm may strike down here. We'll go as far as we can to-night."

CHAPTER VII
A QUEER SAIL

NOW that the fear and worriment was over they all began to feel hungry, and, while Mark and Jack took charge of the conning tower Washington got breakfast. The professor seemed preoccupied during the meal, and several times, when Mark spoke to him, he did not reply.

"I wonder if he is worried about something, or is thinking of something which seems to be concealed in the storeroom," the boy thought.

But, after a while, the professor seemed to be more like himself. He was busy over several maps and charts, and then announced the ship would try air-sailing again for a while.

"We can make better time above than we can on the water," he said, "and I am anxious to get to the mysterious island and learn what is in store for us."

Perhaps if the professor had been able to look ahead, and see what was soon going to happen, he would not have been so anxious for it to occur.

It was shortly after dinner when, the gas container having been filled, the ship rose in the air, and began sailing over the ocean, about a mile up. The day was a fine one, and, as they were moving south, it was constantly growing warmer. Down on the water, in fact, it was quite hot, but in the air it was just right.

Like some immense bird the Mermaid went flying through the air. The boys and the professor sat upon the deck in easy chairs. It was like being on the top of some tall "sky-scraper" building which, by some strange power, was being moved forward. Below them the ocean tumbled in long, lazy swells.

Suddenly Mark, who was looking through a telescope at the expanse of water stretched out under them, gave a cry.

"There's a ship! She's on fire!"

"Where?" asked the professor, stretching out his hand for the glass.

"Just to the port of the forward tube. See the smoke!" exclaimed Mark.

Mr. Henderson looked. Through the lens he saw a column of black vapor rising skyward. Mingled with it were red flames.

"Lower the Mermaid!" he cried. "We must save those on board if we can!"

Mark ran to the conning tower, where Washington was, to give the order. The colored man, who was looking ahead, intent on guiding the ship, did not at first hear what Mark called.

"Lower us! Send the Mermaid down!" Mark cried again.

The sudden shout, and the excited voice of Mark so startled Washington, that, fearing some accident had happened, he pulled the lever, controlling the gas supply, with more force than necessary.

There was a loud explosion, followed by a crackling sound, a flash of light, and the Mermaid came to a sudden stop.

"What's the matter?" cried Mark, feeling that something was wrong.

"I don't know!" Washington replied, as he dashed toward the engine room.

The Mermaid, her forward flight checked, hung in the air, suspended, neither rising or falling.

"Why don't we go on down?" the professor asked, hurrying to the tower.

"There has been an explosion-- an accident!" exclaimed Mark. "I guess we can't go down!"

"But we must!" Mr. Henderson insisted, seizing the lever which should have produced a downward motion. The handle swung to and fro. It was disconnected from the apparatus it operated.

The ship was now stationary in the air, moving neither forward nor backward, neither rising nor falling. Washington had stopped the air pumps as soon as he learned something was wrong.

When Mr. Henderson saw the useless lever, which had controlled the outlet of gas from the holder, he ran out on deck. One glance told him what had happened. One of the electric wires had become short-circuited,-- that is, the insulation had worn off and allowed the current to escape. This had produced a spark, which had exploded the gas which was in the pipe leading from the generator up into the aluminum holder. Fortunately there was an automatic cut-off for the supply of vapor, or the whole tank would have gone up.

As it was, only a small quantity had blown up, but this was enough to break the machinery at the point where the lever in the conning tower joined the pipe. If it had not been for the automatic cut-off all the gas in the holder would have poured out in a great volume, and the ship would have fallen like a shot.

"Can we do nothing to save those on the burning vessel?" asked Mark, pointing to where a cloud of smoke hung over the ocean.

"I fear not, now," answered the professor. "We are in a bad plight ourselves."

"Are we in any danger?" asked Jack.

"Not specially," Mr. Henderson replied. "But we must find a means of lowering ourselves gradually."

"Then it will be too late to save any of those on the ship," observed Mark.

"I'm afraid so," the scientist made reply.

The Mermaid rested some distance above the surface of the waters. She moved slightly to and fro with the wind, and rocked gently. The professor was examining the broken machinery.

"I have a plan!" suddenly cried Mark.

"What is it?" asked Mr. Henderson.

"Can't we bore a hole in the tank, insert a small faucet or tap, and let the gas out that way gradually?" asked the boy. "When we get down we can rescue those in danger of fire, and, later, can repair the break."

"The very thing!" exclaimed Mr. Henderson. "I never thought of that! Here, Washington! Bring me a drill, and a small stop-cock!"

The drill was obtained from the engine room. Working rapidly Mr. Henderson bored a hole in the lower part of the holder. As soon as the metal was penetrated the gas, which was under considerable pressure, rushed from the tank with a hissing sound. At once the Mermaid began to settle rapidly.

But the professor was prepared for this. He thrust the end of the stop-cock into the hole. It was screwed fast and the valve turned. This stopped the flow of gas and checked the descent of the ship. Then, by opening the tap the vapor was allowed to escape gradually, bringing the Flying Mermaid gently to the water.

As the adventurers approached they could see that the vessel was now a mass of flames. The wind was driving the fire toward the forecastle, and the crew had sought refuge aft. But this expedient could not last long, for, already the tongues of fire were licking the sides of the craft and coming nearer and nearer the seemingly doomed men. The vessel was a large one, and heavily laden.

As those in peril caught sight of the Mermaid settling down into the water, apparently from the clouds, their fears gave place to astonishment. So great was this that they ceased their cries of terror. Then, as they saw that the strange craft navigated the ocean, for the engines were started aboard the Mermaid, they began to call for help.

CHAPTER VIII
THE FLYING MERMAID DISABLED

WE'LL save you!" shouted Mr. Henderson, who was on the deck, while Mark was steering the craft. "Hold on a few minutes longer and we'll be alongside!"

"They're real! They're real!" some of those aboard the burning ship could be heard to shout. Evidently more than one of them had taken the Mermaid for a delusion of their fear-crazed brain.

"They are real persons!" they called again and again. "They are coming to save us!"

Mr. Henderson ran his ship as near the burning craft as he dared. Then he called to the crew to leap into the water and swim to him. He, with Washington, Jack, Bill and Tom, stood ready to haul aboard any who were too weak to help themselves.

In a few minutes all of those left alive on the sailing vessel-- fourteen in all-- had come safely aboard the Mermaid. The ship was now completely enveloped in flames.

"Are there any more left on her?" asked Mr. Henderson of one who appeared to be a mate of the burning craft.

"Not a soul!" was the answer. "The captain and ten men perished in the flames. The fire broke out a week ago in the lower hold. We fought it as well as we could but it got the best of us. Then it suddenly broke through the decks, almost like an explosion, a little while ago, and the captain and others were lost, and so were our small boats. We managed to get aft but were about to give up when you appeared."

"What ship is it and where are you from?"

"The Good Hope, laden with logwood, hides, jute and other materials from South America," the mate answered. "We were bound for New York."

"It is more like the Last Hope instead of the Good Hope," observed Mr. Henderson in a quiet voice, as he saw the flames mount higher and higher over the ship. A few seconds later the craft seemed rent by an internal explosion. It appeared to break in two parts, and, amid a shower of sparks and a cloud of black smoke, the vessel sank under the water and was seen no more.

The rescued men turned to behold the final end of their ship. They betrayed no particular emotion, and some of them even laughed, which the professor thought, at the time, was rather strange. But there was little opportunity for speculation. The men were in a sad plight. Few of them had more than the clothes they stood in, though each one wore about his waist a belt, and all of them seemed to guard the leather circlets jealously.

The professor and his crew were soon busy supplying remedies for burns, since several of the men were seared by the flames. Then, as it was learned they had eaten nothing for many hours, it having been impossible to use the galley, a meal was prepared and the survivors of the wreck were well fed.

The hunger of the newcomers having been appeased, they showed much curiosity over the strange craft that had so opportunely come to their rescue. Most of the sailors were ignorant men, and the professor had little fear of them learning anything concerning his secrets. He explained briefly about the Mermaid, but said nothing of whither she was bound.

The addition of fourteen men to the rather small accommodations of the Mermaid was a serious matter to consider. The ship was able to hold them all, and even to sail through the air with them, since Mr. Henderson had provided an excess of power. But it was going to be a problem to feed so many, and still save enough provisions, for the long voyage which lay ahead.

However, Mr. Henderson felt his first duty to be toward his fellowmen, even if his voyage must be delayed, or given up for a time, while he got more provisions. There would be no sleeping quarters for the sailors, but when this was explained to them they cheerfully said they would sleep on deck if necessary. In fact some of them had to, but as the weather was warm and clear this was no hardship. A few found quarters in the engine room and other apartments of the Mermaid.

Finding, after an examination, that his ship was in good order save for the broken gas apparatus, Mr. Henderson gave orders to proceed along the surface of the ocean. The sailors wanted to see how it felt to mount into the air, but Mr. Henderson, refused to attempt a flight until he had made complete repairs, and this would take a day or more.

At this there appeared to be some discontent among the survivors, and they muttered to each other as they stood in a group on deck. But the professor and his assistants were too busy with their preparations for fixing the break to notice this.

While the men were gathered in a knot near the after part of the small deck, the mate separated from them, and, coming close to where Mark was standing, unscrewing some of the broken parts of the pipe said, in a low voice.

"Tell the captain to watch out."

"What do you mean?" asked Mark quickly.

"Hush! Not so loud!" the mate exclaimed. "If the men hear me talking to you, or see me, they may kill me. Tell the captain to look out; that's all. Be on guard, and watch the engine room carefully."

"But why-- ?" Mark began, when, turning suddenly, the mate left him. It was well he did so, for, at that instant, one of the sailors, who had observed the two conversing, strolled in their direction.

Much alarmed, Mark sought Mr. Henderson and told him what he had heard.

"I suppose the fire may have turned the poor man's head," the scientist said. "I wonder if he thinks the men I rescued would mutiny and take possession of my ship? If they did they would not know how to work it, so what good would it do?"

"Hadn't we better look out?" asked Mark.

"I'm not afraid," replied the professor. "I will be too busy the next few days, repairing the break, to think of anything else. Besides, what would they want to harm us for? Didn't we save their lives?"

Seeing the scientist placed no faith in what the mate had said, Mark went back to his task.

It soon became too dark to work, and it was decided, after supper, to halt the ship until morning as it would be less risky.

Mark did not sleep well, his dreams being disturbed by visions of pirates and black flags. But morning came and nothing had developed. The men seemed to recover their spirits with daybreak, and mast of the crew, after breakfast, greeted Mr. Henderson pleasantly, and asked to be allowed to help fix the ship.

It took the skilled labor of the professor, Washington and the boys to mend the break, and, even at that, it was four days in the repairing. But at last the final bolt was in place, and the Mermaid was able to resume her trips through the air.

"We will rise the first thing in the morning," said the professor to Mark and Jack that night. "I am anxious to see how the ship behaves with a big load aboard."

CHAPTER IX
THE MUTINY

MARK was awakened that night by feeling some one trying to turn him over. At first he thought it was Jack, and sleepily muttered that he wanted to be let alone.

"Sorry I can't oblige ye, my hearty!" exclaimed a rough voice in his ear, "but I got particular orders t' tie you up!"

At that Mark tried to sit up, but he found he could not. He discovered that he was closely bound with many turns of a rope, while in front of his bunk stood one of the rescued sailors.

"There," said the man, with a final tightening of the ropes. "I guess you're safe."

"What's the matter? What does it all mean?" asked Mark, much bewildered.

"It means that we have possession of the ship," the sailor answered, "and, if you're wise you'll not make a fuss. It wouldn't do any good, anyhow, as all your friends are in the same condition."

Then, picking Mark up, as if he was a baby, the man slung him over his shoulder and carried him to the living room. There Mark saw Jack, the professor, Washington, and the others similarly bound.

"Do you realize what you are doing?" asked the professor angrily of his captors. "You are mutinying, and are liable to severe punishment."

"If they ever get us," added one of the men. "We've got the ship now, and we mean to keep her. You'll have to run her or show us how."

"Never!" cried the professor.

"I guess he will when he feels this," said one of the men, as he dragged from a recess two wires. "I happen to know something of electricity, and when he feels these perhaps he'll change his mind. I'll start the dynamo."

The sailor showed that he was acquainted with machinery, for soon the hum of the electric apparatus was heard.

"Now to make him tell!" the man with the wires exclaimed, advancing toward the professor, who turned pale.

"Stop! You must not torture the old man!" cried a voice, and the mate of the Good Hope stepped in front of the sailor with the electrified wires.

"Who's going to stop me?" asked the man.

"I will. It's not necessary," the mate went on quickly. "If we make him weak we may kill him, and he can not tell us what we want to know. One of the boys can tell us how to run the ship."

The mate came quickly over to where Mark lay, and whispered:

"Consent to tell. It is the only way of saving his life. Tell 'em how to raise the craft. Then leave all to me. I will save you all and the ship, too, if I can. But consent."

Mark nodded his head, and the mate cried:

"I knew I could fetch 'em. I have hypnotic power. This boy will raise the ship for us. Loosen his bonds, some of you."

Satisfied that they were now on the way to experiencing a new sensation, the sailors took the ropes off Mark's arms and legs, and he was allowed to rise. With a reassuring nod toward the professor he led the way to the engine room, followed by half the men. He resolved to start the gas machine slowly, so as to make the upward trip last longer, thinking before it had gone far, some way of escape from the mutineers might be found.

While a crowd of the sailors stood near him, Mark operated the machinery in the engine room that started the gas generating, and set the negative gravity apparatus working.

"You'd better not try any tricks on us," said one of the men in an ugly tone of voice.

"I'm not going to," replied Mark. "If you go out on deck you will soon see the ship leaving the water and mounting into the air."

"Some of you go," ordered a man with a big bushy red beard. "See if the ship rises. When she begins to go up sing out. I'm going to stay here and see how the young cub does it so I can work it myself."

Obeying the red-bearded man, who seemed to be a leader, several of the sailors went out on the deck. It was quite dark, but there was a phosphorous glow to the water which made the rolling waves visible.

The gas was being generated, as could be told by the hissing sound. Mark watched the machinery anxiously, for he knew much depended on him, and the professor was not at hand to guide and instruct him. He watched the dial of the gage which registered the gas pressure and saw it slowly moving. In a little while it would be at the point at which the ship ought to rise.

Presently a quiver seemed to run through the Mermaid. Now a shout came from the watchers on deck.

"She's going up!"

The ship was indeed rising. The red-bearded man, who was addressed as Tony, ran from the engine room to the deck. He saw that the ship was now ten feet above the water. Back he came to where Mark stood by the gas machine.

"Lucky for you that you didn't fool us, lad," he said with a leer. "See that you mind me hereafter. Now show me how the shebang works."

When the ship had risen as far as Tony desired he made Mark send it straight ahead. The boy adjusted the air tube to carry the craft toward the south, but Tony, seeing by a compass in which direction they were headed, ordered Mark to steer due east.

"Fix things so they will stay so, too," added Tony. "I don't want to stop until I get a thousand miles away. Then we'll come down, sail to some sunny island, and enjoy life."

Mark locked the steering apparatus so as to keep the Mermaid headed due east.

"Now you can go back to your friends," Tony said. "When I want you I'll send for you."

With a heavy heart Mark rejoined the professor and others. He found them with their bonds removed. But to guard against their escape several men were on watch outside the door.

"What are they doing?" asked the professor eagerly as Mark entered, and the boy told him what had taken place.

"They will ruin my ship and spoil the whole trip," cried the old scientist. "Oh, why did I ever go to the rescue of the scoundrels?"

"Never mind," said Jack. "Perhaps we may yet outwit them."

Morning came at last. The ship was still shooting forward at fast speed, in an easterly direction. The sailors had learned, in their short stay aboard, where the food and stores were kept, and they lost little time in getting breakfast. They sent same in to their captives, including a big pot of hot coffee, and, after partaking of this the professor and his friends felt better.

The mate of the Good Hope came in to help clear away the dishes. As he passed Mark he slipped into the boy's hand a note.

"Don't read it until you are alone," he said in a low voice, as he hurried from the room.

As soon as the other sailors had left, Mark glanced at the slip of paper. It bore these words:

"Open when you hear three raps, then two, then three, and keep silent."

"What is it?" asked Mr. Henderson.

Mark showed him the paper.

"I wonder what it means," the boy said.

"Do you think he is a friend of ours?" the professor asked.

Mark told him of the mate's conversation the night previous.

"I think we can trust him," the scientist went on. "He must intend to pay us a visit when the others are asleep. When we hear the knocks as he specifies we must open the door and let him in."

All that day the captives were kept in the living room. Once or twice Mark was sent for to make some adjustment to the machinery, but the apparatus, for the most part, was automatic, and needed little attention. The professor, as well as the others, were all impatience for the promised visit of the mate. Still they felt he would not come until night.

In fact it was long past midnight before Mark, Jack and the professor, who were anxiously listening, heard the three raps, then two, then three more. Mark quickly opened the door, and the mate stepped inside, holding his finger to his lips as a sign of caution. Old Andy, Washington, Bill and Tom had fallen asleep.

"I have only time for a few words," the mate said. "I am closely watched. Tony mistrusts me. I will save you if I can."

"Why have they repaid my kindness with such actions?" asked Mr. Henderson.

"Because they are desperate men," replied the mate. "They are nothing more than pirates. They mutinied on the other ship, killed the captain and those of the crew who would not join them, and started off to seek their fortunes. I pretended to join them to save my life, but I have only been watching for a chance to escape.

"Because of lax discipline the ship was sent on fire. We tried to put it out but could not. The rest you know."

"I heard them plan to capture this airship, but could do nothing to stop them. Then I resolved to pretend to act with them. They fear pursuit for their other mutiny, and are anxious to get as far away as possible."

"Do you think they will abandon the ship in a little while?" asked the professor hopefully.

"I'm afraid not," answered the mate. "I think they want to get rid of all of you, so they can sail about as they please. Tony is a smart man. He could soon learn to run this ship, he thinks."

"I doubt it," Mr. Henderson answered. "But how are you going to help us?"

"I have not fully made up my plans," the mate answered. "However I wanted you to know I would do my best to save you. Now I must go. Be on the watch and when I can I will let you know what I have decided on. I will hand Mark a note when I bring your meals, just as I did to-day. I think----"

"Hark! What was that?" asked the professor.

There was a noise outside the door, as if some one was listening.

"Put out the lights!" whispered the mate, and Jack switched off the electric incandescents.

A knock sounded on the door and the voice of Tony called:

"Mark! Come here! I want you to look at the gas machine. It has stopped working, and we are falling!"

CHAPTER X
FOOLING THEIR ENEMIES

MARK hurried into the corridor, taking care to close the door after him, so Tony could get no glimpse of the mate who had risked so much to save his friends. But he need not have been alarmed for the leader of the mutineers was too excited over the stopping of the gas apparatus to give any heed to who was in with the captives.

"Do you think you can fix it?" he asked the boy.

"I guess so," Mark replied confidently. "If I can't there is no danger, for we will fall gradually and land in the water."

"But I don't want to do that," Tony objected. "I want to keep on through the air."

Mark did not reply. By this time he was at the gas machine. He soon saw nothing was the matter save that new material must be placed in the retort where the vapor was generated. He refilled it, the gas was manufactured once more, and the ship began to rise.

"I will know how to do it next time," Tony said with a grin. Mark realized that every time he showed the leader of the mutineers something about the ship it was putting the professor and his friends more and more into the power of the scoundrels. But there was no help for it.

The ship was still plunging ahead, and kept about a mile above the earth. As there was no further need of Mark, he was told he could go back to his friends. When he reached the room where they were held prisoners, he found the mate had gone away, promising again to do all he could for them.

The next night, which it seemed would never come, for the day, locked as the captives were in their room, seemed endless, finally closed in. Mark, Jack and the professor were anxious to know whether the mate would pay them another visit. As for Andy, Tom and Bill, while they were interested in the ship, and wanted to be free from the power of the mutineers, they did not lose any sleep over it.

Shortly after midnight, there came again the peculiar knock, and the mate entered the room. He seemed much excited over something, and, as soon as the portal was securely closed he said to Professor Henderson:

"Is there an island any where near here where men could live for a time?"

"What do you mean?" asked the scientist. "Do you want us to desert the ship and leave these scoundrels in charge?"

"Nothing of the sort," replied the mate, who, had said his name was Jack Rodgers. "But first answer my question. A great deal may depend on it."

Seeing Rodgers was in earnest, the professor looked over some maps and charts, and announced that they were within a few hundred miles of a group of islands.

"When would we reach them?" was Rodgers's next question.

Mr. Henderson made a few rapid calculations on a piece of paper.

"At the present rate of sailing," he said, "we should be there about ten o'clock to-morrow. That is, provided the ship does not slacken speed or increase it."

"There is no danger of either of those two things happening," said the mate. "Tony is too afraid of the machinery to do anything to it. So you may safely figure that our speed will continue the same."

"Then I can guarantee, with all reasonable certainty," the professor said, "that about ten o'clock to-morrow we will be less than a mile from the islands. They are a group where friendly natives live, and where many tropical fruits abound. One could scarcely select a better place to be shipwrecked. But I hope the plans of Tony and his friends do not include landing us there."

"No, nothing like that," the mate answered. "Quite the contrary. But I had better be going. I will try and see Mark some time to-morrow. Tony does not mind when I speak to him."

With this Rodgers left the captives, as he heard some of the sailors moving about and did not want to be discovered. The professor and the boys wondered what the mate's plan might be, but they had to be content to wait and see.

The night passed without incident. About nine o'clock the next morning the mate came to the door of the room where the professor and his friends were prisoners. He made no secret of his approach, but knocked boldly.

"Tell Mark I want to see him," he said, as the professor answered. "All of you keep quiet," he added in a whisper. "There may be good news soon."

Mark slipped from the room. He followed the mate to the upper deck which, at that time was deserted as all the sailors were in the dining room eating, which practice they indulged in as often as they could.

"I have a plan to get rid of these rough men," the mate said to Mark. "It may work, and, again it may not. At any rate it is worth trying, It all depends on you with what help I can give you."

"I'm willing to do my share," Mark said, and for the next ten minutes the boy and the mate were in earnest conversation.

It was about thirty-five minutes later when there arose a sudden commotion in the ship. Mark had returned to his friends and the mate had disappeared. The confusion seemed to come from the engine room where Tony had posted some of his men.

"We're falling down! We'll all be killed!" shouted the men. "The ship is falling into the sea!"

"What is the trouble?" asked the professor as he heard the commotion.

"It is part of the mate's plan," said Mark. "He told me to tell you to do nothing. If Tony or any of the other men come to you just refer them to me."

Two minutes later Tony came rushing into the apartment where the captives were held prisoners.

"Here! Come quickly, Mark!" he exclaimed. "Something has gone wrong with the gas machine again, and you must come and fix it before we are all dashed to pieces!"

With every appearance of haste Mark rushed from the apartment, following Tony. The latter led the way to the engine room.

"Can anything be done?" he asked.

Mark took a survey of the machinery.

"It is too late," he said as though much excited. "The ship is falling down toward the sea with terrific force."

It needed but a glance at the height gage to show this. The pointer was revolving rapidly about the face of the dial.

"Will the ship stand the blow?" asked Tony.

"Not at the rate it is falling," replied Mark. "She will go all to pieces when she strikes the water, and she may explode!"

"What are we to do then?" asked the leader of the mutineers.

"We must save ourselves!" cried the mate, running in at this juncture. "Let our prisoners shift for themselves as best they can. Let's all leap into the sea. There we at least have a chance for our lives. But if we stay on this ship we will all be drowned like cats in a bag."

"What do you propose?" asked Tony, his face white with fear.

"When the ship comes near enough the surface of the water to make it safe we should all drop overboard!" the mate exclaimed. "We are near some islands, I understand, and we can thus save our lives by swimming ashore."

This plan seemed to meet with instant favor, and a little later there was a rush for the deck, as each one wished to be the first to escape from the boat they believed to be doomed.

Lower and lower fell the Mermaid. She was like a wounded bird which the shot of the hunter has crippled. Down and down she fluttered.

By this time all the sailors, save the mate were on deck. He and Mark remained in the engine room.

"Don't let her get too low," the mate whispered.

"I'll watch out," Mark replied. "I want to give them a good scare while I'm at it."

The ship was now within fifty feet of the water. There was a cry of terror from the sailors. Some of them leaped over the rail and started to swim ashore, as the ship was by this time close to a group of islands.

Suddenly, from the engine room the mate rushed.

"Jump! Jump for your lives!" he exclaimed. "The ship is about to blow up!"

CHAPTER XI
MYSTERIOUS HAPPENINGS

THE voice of the mate echoed through the Mermaid. Those on deck heard it, as did Tony in the engine room, where he was vainly trying to understand the complicated machinery.

An instant later there sounded from beneath the ship a series of splashes. More sailors were leaping from the deck of the craft to the ocean. The distance was not great, particularly as they all landed in water.

"Quick!" cried the mate to a group of sailors that hesitated before taking the jump. "The ship may blow up any minute now."

The men needed no second urging. As soon as they struck the water they began to swim ashore, as it was not far away. One after another they jumped over the rail. Tony was the last to go. He urged the captives to follow him, but they all refused.

A minute later the only one of the pirate crew left on the ship was the mate. The others were all struggling in the sea. Eventually they all reached shore in safety.

The airship was now within about twenty feet of the water. It was still falling but not so rapidly.

"Better send her up, now," said the mate to Mark, and the boy turned the necessary levers to accomplish this.

Dipping into the water as a sea gull does when searching for food on the wing, for she had come quite low, the Mermaid mounted once more into the air, and was soon sailing along over the heads of Tony and his gang.

"What's it all about?" asked Mr. Henderson, who seemed in a sort of stupor. "I thought the ship was broken. How, then, can it rise?"

"It was only a trick of mine," Rodgers said. "The gas machine is not broken. I had Mark fix it so that only a little vapor would be generated. When the supply in the holder was not enough, and no more was being made, the ship had to sink. Mark and I pretended it was worse than it really was just to scare the scoundrels."

"And you evidently succeeded," observed Mr. Henderson. "They have all left us. I am glad you stayed."

"So am I," said Rodgers. "I was just waiting for a chance to escape from that crowd. This was the plan I thought of that night. I wanted to see the men put on some island where they could manage to live, and which was not too far away."

The Mermaid was now mounting upward rapidly, as Mark had adjusted the machinery properly. The craft was well rid of the pirate crew, and was able to proceed on its way, and enable Mr. Henderson to carry out his plans.

When the Mermaid had reached a certain height her prow was turned the other way, and she was sent back racing over the ground she had just covered. But now the ship was in the hands of friends. Fortunately no great damage had been done by the sailors, and the professor was soon able to get things in ship-shape. The engines had not been molested and were working better than ever.

"Now to make another attempt to reach the big hole in the earth," the professor cried. "We will be careful next time, who we rescue from ships at sea."

The island was soon left behind, becoming a mere speck on the ocean. Those aboard the Mermaid knew no harm could befall the sailors, as there were no savage tribes on the little spot of land. Eventually the sailors were picked up by a passing vessel and taken to their homes. The story of their first mutiny leaked out and they were properly punished.

It required several days travel before the airship regained the distance she had lost because of the plans of the pirates. Also, there were a number of minor repairs to make, and the professor and his friends were kept busy.

"How much longer before we come to the big hole?" asked Jack, one day.

"I think we ought to be near it in about two weeks," the professor replied. "I only hope we shall not be disappointed, and will be able to explore it."

"'Tain't goin' t' be no fun t' be decimated an' expurgitated inter a conglomerous aggregation of elements constituting th' exterior portion of human anatomy," said Washington in dubious tones.

"You mean you're afraid of being boiled in the steam from the big hole?" asked Mark.

"Jest so," replied the colored man.

"You don't need to worry about that," put in the professor. "I will not take the ship down if there is any danger, though of course there will be some risk."

The ship, having been fully repaired, was now able to be speeded up, and was sent scudding along toward her destination. Rodgers proved a valuable acquisition toward the crew, for he had sailed many years in the waters over which they were flying, and was able to give the professor many valuable hints. He had heard vague stories of the island with the big hole, but had never been near it. He did not make the trip however, as, at his request, he was put off at an inhabited island one night.

It was about a week after the sailors were frightened from the ship, that a curious experience befell Mark. Washington was on duty in the conning tower, attending to the apparatus as the ship flew through the air, and all the others had gone to bed. Mark had remained up, later than the others as he was interested in reading a book on science.

About ten o'clock he became hungry, and going to the pantry got some bread and cold meat. He set these on a table, and then, remembering he would need some water to drink, started after some in the cooler, which was in a little room near the tower.

Washington heard the boy as he turned the faucet to draw the liquid, and spoke to him, as the colored man was rather lonesome at his post. Mark did not linger more than a minute or two, but when he returned to where he had left the food he was much surprised.

There was not a trace of it to be seen. The dishes were on the table, but every vestige of bread and meat had disappeared.

"I wonder if a cat or dog has been here," was Mark's first thought. Then he remembered that no such animals were aboard the Mermaid.

Something on the floor caught his eye. He stooped and picked it up. It was a slice of bread, but in such shape that the boy stared at it, puzzled as to how it could have become so.

It was flattened out quite thin, but the strangest part of it was that it bore what seemed to be the marks of thumb and fingers from a very large hand. So big, in fact, was the print, that Mark's hand scarce covered half of it, and, where the bread had been squeezed into a putty like mass (for it was quite fresh) the peculiar markings on the skin of the tips of the fingers were visible.

"It looks as if a giant grabbed this slice of bread," Mark observed. "There are strange happenings aboard this ship. I wish I knew what they meant."

He looked all around for the food, thinking perhaps a rat had dragged it off, but there was no trace of it.

Suddenly the boy thought he heard a sound from the big storeroom. He was almost sure he heard something moving in there. He started toward the door when he was stopped by hearing the professor's voice call:

"Don't open that door, Mark. Have I not told you that place must not be entered?"

"I thought I heard some one in there," Mark replied.

"There is nothing in there but some apparatus of mine," Mr. Henderson said. "I want no one to see it. What is the matter?"

Mark explained matters to the scientist, who had, as he said later, arisen on hearing the boy, moving about.

"Oh, it was a rat that took your stuff," Mr. Henderson said. "I guess there are some pretty big ones on the ship. Get some more food and go to sleep."

Mark felt it best to obey, though he was by no means satisfied with the professor's explanation. He listened intently to see if any more noises came from the storeroom, but none did, and he went to bed.

Several times after that Mark tried the experiment of leaving food about. On each occasion it was taken.

"It looks as if the ship was haunted," he said. "Of course I know it isn't, but it's very queer. They must be strange rats that can get food from shelves when there is only the smooth side of the ship to climb up," for on some occasions Mark had tried the experiment of putting the food as nearly out of reach as possible.

It took several nights to learn all this, and, as he did not want to take any one into his confidence, he had to work in secret. But, with all his efforts he learned nothing, save that there was something odd about the ship that he could not fathom.

At first he believed the professor had some strange animal concealed in the storeroom, but he dismissed this idea almost as soon as he thought of it. For what could the scientist want with an animal when they were going to the interior of the earth? That some beast had slipped aboard was out of the question. Mark was much puzzled, but finally, deciding the matter did not concern him a great deal, gave up trying to solve the mystery, at least for a time.

The ship was now in the neighborhood of the equator and the climate had become much warmer. So hot indeed were some nights that they slept out on deck, with the Mermaid flying through the air at a moderate pace, for it was deemed best not to go at any great speed after dark.

One night the professor, after consulting various charts and maps, and making calculations which covered several sheets of paper announced:

"We should sight the mysterious island to-morrow."

"That's good news!" exclaimed Jack. "I'm anxious to see what's below inside of that big hole."

"Everybody git ready for their funerals!" exclaimed Washington in a deep voice. "I ain't got many----"

"Cheer up," interrupted Jack, poking Washington in the ribs. The colored man was very ticklish, and he began to laugh heartily, though, perhaps, he did not feel like it.

Suddenly, above the sound of his shouts, there came a crashing, grinding noise from the engine room.

CHAPTER XII
THE BIG HOLE

SOMETHING has gone wrong!" exclaimed the professor as he jumped up. He reached the engine room ahead of any one else, and when the two boys got there they found him busy twisting wheels and shifting levers.

"Anything serious?" asked Jack.

"It's the gas machine again," Mr. Henderson replied. "It broke where we fixed it. However it doesn't matter. I was going to lower the ship anyhow, as I want to approach the island from the water. We will go down a little sooner than I counted on."

The disabling of the gas machine caused the vapor to escape slowly from the tank, and this made the ship sink gradually. By means of the emergency stop-cock the descent could be controlled almost as well as though the machinery was in working order. Half an hour later the Mermaid rested on the water.

It was a little rough, as there was quite a swell on, and not so pleasant as floating in the air on an even keel, but they made the best of it.

On account of the little accident, and not being certain of its extent, it was deemed best not to send the ship ahead. So they laid to until morning.

For the better part of two days all those on board the Mermaid had their hands full mending the break and making other repairs found necessary. In that time they lay to, floating idly with the currents, or blown by the wind, for the professor would not start any of the engines or apparatus until the ship was in good condition.

In this time Mark had several times recalled the curious happenings in regard to the disappearing food, and the mystery of the storeroom. But there were no further manifestations, and no other signs that there might be a strange visitor aboard.

"I couldn't have imagined it all," said Mark, "but I guess what did happen may have been caused by natural means, only I can't discover them."

It was about two days after this, the ship having sailed scores of miles on the surface of the water, that Mark, who was in the conning tower exclaimed:

"That looks like a waterspout ahead of us."

"That's what it is!" Jack agreed. "What shall we do?"

"Call the professor!" said Mark. "He'll know."

When Mr. Henderson came, he looked for a long time at a cloud of black vapor which hung low in the east.

"It may be a waterspout," he said. "We'll rise in the air and see if we can avoid it."

The ship was sent up into the air. As it rose higher and higher, the professor, making frequent observations from his conning tower, cried out:

"That is no waterspout!"

"What is it?" asked Mark.

"It is the steam and vapor rising from the big hole in the earth! Boys, we are almost there!"

"Are you sure that's it?" asked Mark.

"Almost positive," Mr. Henderson replied. "You can see how much warmer it has become of late, as we approached the equator. We are almost due at the island, and I have no doubt we have reached it."

As the ship flew forward the mass of dark vapor became more pronounced. Through the glasses it could be noticed to consist of rolling masses of clouds. What lay beneath them no one knew. The adventurers were going to try to find out.

Now that they had arrived at the beginning of the main part of their journey, the travelers felt their spirits sink a little. It was one thing to plan to go down into the depths of the earth, but it was quite another to make the actual attempt. Still, they were not going to give up the project. The professor had confidence in his ship and believed it could safely make the trip. Still it was with no little apprehension that Mr. Henderson watched the nearer approach of the craft to that strange island.

"Perfesser, are yo' really an' truly goin' t' depress this elongated spheroid an' its human consignment int' that conglomerous convoluted mass of gaseous vapor regardless of th' consequences?" asked Washington, as he gazed with wide opened eyes at the sight before him.

"If you mean am I going to let the Mermaid go down into that hole you are perfectly correct," the scientist answered, "though you could have said it in fewer words, Washington."

"I-- I guess I'll get out an' walk," the colored man made reply.

"This isn't any trolley car," observed Mark. "Don't lose your nerve, Wash. Stay with us, and we'll discover a gold or diamond mine, maybe."

"Is there diamonds down there?" asked the colored man, his fright seeming to leave him.

"There are all sorts of things inside the earth," the professor answered.

"Then I'm goin' along!" Washington declared. "I always did want a diamond ring, an' I knows a little colored gal that wants one, too. I'm goin' all right! This suttenly am th' most kloslosterous conjunctivity of combativeness that I ever sagaciated!" and he began to do a sort of impromptu cake-walk.

CHAPTER XIII
DOWN INTO THE EARTH

IT was now noon, but the adventurers did not think of dinner in the excitement of approaching the mysterious island. The speed of the ship was increased that they might the more quickly come to it. As they approached they could see the masses of vapor more plainly, and it appeared that some great commotion must be going on inside the big hole, since clouds of steam arose.

"I only hope it doesn't prove too hot for us," observed the professor. "However, I provided a water jacket for the ship, and we may need it, as well as the vacuum chambers to keep the heat from us."

It was about three o'clock when the flying ship reached the edge of the island. From there it was about a mile to the rim of the big hole, over one side of which the waters of the ocean poured with a roar that could be heard over half a mile off.

"I think we had better halt and see that everything is in good shape before proceeding," said Mr. Henderson. "Jack, you and Mark make a thorough inspection of the engine room, and see that all the apparatus is in working order,"

The two boys prepared to do as they were told. Mark, who was walking a little ahead of Jack, entered the apartment from which the storeroom opened. As he did so he saw, or thought he saw, the door of the place where the extra supplies were kept, close. Without saying anything to Jack he hurried forward, and tried the knob. It would not turn.

"That's funny," said Mark to himself. "I could almost swear I saw some one go into that room. Yet I know the professor did not enter, for I just left him. And none of the others would dare to. I wonder if I will ever solve the mystery."

But he had too much to do to allow him to dwell on that matter. Several of the dynamos needed adjusting and for two hours he and Jack had all they could do.

In the meanwhile the professor had gone over the other parts of the ship, and gotten everything in readiness for the descent. The Mermaid was lowered to within a few hundred feet of the sea, and, through a hose that was let down, the compartments, provided for this emergency were filled with water. These compartments were between the outer and inner hulls of the lower part of the craft, and were designed to prevent the interior becoming heated in case the travelers found they had to pass close to fire. There were also vacuum chambers, and from these the air was exhausted, as of course every schoolboy knows a vacuum is a non-conductor of either heat or cold.

"Now I think we are ready," the professor announced at length.

"Everything's all right in the engine room," announced Jack.

"Yes, an' everything's all right in th' kitchen," put in Washington. "I've got a good meal ready as soon as any one wants to eat."

"It will have to wait a while," Mr. Henderson remarked. "We are going to start to make the descent before we dine."

The hose was reeled up, and the ship was sent a few hundred feet higher into the air, as Mr. Henderson wanted to take a last good observation before he went down into the hole.

But having risen some distance above the masses of rolling vapors he found he was at no advantage, since the strongest telescope he could bring to bear could not pierce the cloud masses.

"We'll just have to trust to luck," the scientist said. "I judge we're about over the centre of the opening. Lower away Mark!"

The boy, who, under the watchful eye of the professor, was manipulating the levers and wheels in the conning tower, shifted some handles. The gas was expelled from the holder, the negative gravity apparatus ceased to work, and the Flying Mermaid sank lower and lower, toward the mysterious hole that yawned beneath her.

The hearts of all beat strangely, if not with fear, at least with apprehension, for they did not know what they might encounter. Perhaps death in some terrible form awaited them. But the desire to discover something new and strange had gripped all of them, and not one would have voted to turn back.

Even old Andy, who seldom got excited, was in unusual spirits. He took down his gun and remarked:

"Maybe I can kill some new kind of animal, and write a book about its habits, for surely we will see strange beasts in the under-world."

Lower and lower sank the ship. Now it was amid the first thin masses of vapors, those that floated highest and were more like a light fog, than anything else. By means of a window in the bottom of the craft, which window was closed by a thick piece of plate glass, Professor Henderson could look down and see what was beneath them.

"The clouds seem to be getting thicker," he said, as he peered through the small casement. "If they would only clear away we could see something."

But instead of doing this the vapors accumulated more thickly about the ship. It was so dark inside the Mermaid now that the electric lights had to be switched on. In the room with the floor-window the lights were not used, as had they shone one could not have seen down below.

The professor maintained his position. The descent was a perilous one, and he wanted to be on the watch to check it at once if the Mermaid was liable to dash upon some pointed rock or fall into some fiery pit. His hand was on the signal levers.

Suddenly he looked up and glanced at a gage on the wall. The hand of it was slowly revolving.

"We are at the earth's surface," the scientist said. "Now we are below it. Now we are fairly within the big hole! Boys, we may be on the verge of a great discovery!"

An instant later it seemed as if a hot wave had struck the Mermaid, or as if the craft had been plunged into boiling water.

"It's going to be hot!" cried the professor. "Lucky I provided the water jackets!"

Then the lights in the interior of the ship went out, leaving the whole craft in darkness.

"What has happened?" cried Mark.

CHAPTER XIV
MANY MILES BELOW

D ON'T be alarmed," spoke the calm voice of the professor. "I have only turned off the electrics. I want to switch on the search lights, to see if we can learn anything about our position."

As he spoke he turned a switch, and, the gloom below the ship, as the boys could see by glimpses from the floor-window, was pierced by a dazzling glare. In the bottom of the Mermaid were set a number of powerful electric arc lights with reflectors, constructed to throw the beams downward. The professor had built them in for just this emergency, as he thought that at some time they might want to illuminate what was below the craft.

Not that it was of much avail on this occasion, for, though the lights were powerful, they could not pierce the miles of gloom that lay below them. The beams only served to accentuate the darkness.

"I guess we'll have to trust to luck," the professor said, after a vain attempt, by means of powerful glasses, to distinguish something. "There is too much fog and vapor."

"What makes it so warm?" asked Mark, removing his coat.

"Well, you must remember you are approaching the interior of the earth," the professor answered. "It has been calculated that the heat increases one degree for every fifty-five feet you descend. We have come down several hundred feet and of course it is getting warmer."

"Then if we go down very far it will get so hot we will not be able to stand it," Jack put in.

"I do not believe we will suffer any great inconvenience," Mr. Henderson went on. "I believe that after we pass a certain point it will become cooler. I think the inner fires of the earth are more or less heated gas in a sort of inner chamber between two shells. If we can pass the second shell, we will be all right."

"But aren't we liable to hit something, going down into the dark this way?" asked Mark.

"We will guard ourselves as far as possible," the scientist answered.

The Mermaid seemed to be going down on a side of the immense shaft a good way distant from the strange waterfall. When they had first dropped into the hole the travelers could hear the rush of waters, but now the noise was not audible.

"I think the hole must widen out the farther down we go," the professor said. "We are probably many miles from the fall now."

"I'm sure I hope so," put in Jack. "It would be no fun to have to take a shower bath in this place."

After a meal, the boys and the professor took some more observations, but with all their efforts nothing could be seen below the ship but a vast black void, into which they were steadily descending.

"I wonder when we're going to stop," asked Mark. "It's like playing the game 'Going to Jerusalem,' you keep wondering when the music will cease and you will have a chance to grab a chair. I only hope we have a chair or something else to sit on, in case we go to smash."

"We're not liable to have any accidents with the professor in charge," Jack answered. "Didn't he bring us safe out of some pretty tight holes when we went to the north pole in the airship, and again when we found the south pole in the submarine?"

"Yes, but this is different," objected Mark.

"Well, I'm not worrying," Jack went on. "It doesn't do any good, and only makes you lie awake nights. By the way, I wonder what time it is getting to be."

He looked at his watch and found it was close on to eight o'clock in the evening. So late had dinner been served, and so varied were the happenings of the last few hours, that time had passed quickly.

"Why it's almost bed-time," said Jack. "I wonder if we are to go on dropping into the depths of nowhere all night."

At that moment the professor entered the room where the boys were. He seemed quite pleased over something, and was smiling.

"Everything is going along famously," he said. "I have just tested the air and find it is rich in oxygen. We shall suffer nothing on that score. The heat too, seems to have decreased. On the whole, everything favors us."

"Are we going on down?" asked Mark.

"As far as we can," Mr. Henderson answered. "Let me see how far we are below now."

He went to the gage that indicated the vertical position of the ship. Because of the changed conditions, the craft now sinking below the surface of the earth instead of rising above it, as was its wont, some calculations were necessary. These the scientist made as quickly as he could.

"We are now ten miles underground!" he exclaimed. "That is doing very well. My theories are working out. I think we shall land somewhere before long."

"I hopes so!" exclaimed Washington coming in at this point. "I'm mighty skeered shootin' down int' this dark hole, and no time-table t' show when we's due t' arrive."

"We ought to land in a couple of days more," the professor answered. "Never mind about worrying Washington, I'll take care of you."

"I hopes so, Perfesser," the colored man said. "I got a little girl waitin' for me back in Georgia, an' I'd like t' see her 'fore I git burned up."

Accompanied by the professor, the boys made a tour of the ship to see that all the machinery and apparatus were in working order. Owing to the changed conditions the negative gravity engine had to be worked at faster speed than usual, since the downward pull of the earth was greater the farther they descended into the interior and they did not want to fall too swiftly. But this was easily provided for, since the professor had made the apparatus capable of standing a great strain.

The ten miles had become fourteen when the professor, finding that everything was in good shape, proposed that the boys go to bed. They, did not want to, though they were sleepy, and they feared to miss some strange sights.

But when the professor had promised to call them in case anything unusual developed, they consented to turn in, and Bill and Tom assumed their duties, which were light enough, now that the ship was merely falling into the immense shaft.

When Mark turned into his bunk he could not go to sleep at once. It may have been the excitement over their new position, or because he had eaten too hearty a supper, but the fact was he remained awake for some time.

While thus tossing restlessly on his bed, wondering what ailed him, he thought he heard a noise in the main apartment out of which the storeroom opened. He crawled softly from his bed, and looked from his stateroom door.

In the light of a shaded electric Mark saw the figure of some one glide across the floor and take refuge in the room, which Professor Henderson always was so particular about.

"I wonder what or who that was," reasoned Mark. "There is some mystery in this. Can the professor have concealed some one on this ship whose presence he does not want to admit? It certainly looks so."

Not wanting to awaken the ship's crew, and remembering what Mr. Henderson had said about any one entering the storeroom, Mark went back to bed, to fall into an uneasy slumber.

"Breakfast!" called Washington breaking in on a fine dream Jack was having about being captain of a company of automobile soldiers. "Last call for breakfast!"

"Hello! Is it morning?" asked Jack.

"Not so's you could notice it," Washington went on. "It's as dark as a stack of black cats and another one throwed in. But breakfast is ready jest the same."

The boys were soon at the table, and learned that nothing of importance had occurred during the night. The Mermaid had been kept going slowly down, and about seven o'clock registered more than fifty miles below the earth's surface.

Still there was no change in the outward surroundings. It remained as black as the interior of Egypt when that country was at its darkest. The powerful electrics could not pierce the gloom. The ship was working well, and the travelers were very comfortable.

Down, down, down, went the Mermaid. The temperature, which had risen to about ninety went back to sixty-nine, and there seemed to be no more danger from the inner fires.

They were now a hundred miles under the surface. But still the professor kept the Mermaid sinking. Every now and again he would take an observation, but only found the impenetrable darkness surrounded them.

"We must arrive somewhere, soon," he muttered.

It was about six o'clock that night that the alarm bell set up a sudden ringing.

The professor who was making some calculations on a piece of paper jumped to his feet, and so did a number of the others.

"We are nearing the bottom!" he cried. "The bell has given us warning!"

CHAPTER XV
IN THE STRANGE DRAUGHT

THE boys ran to attend to the engines and apparatus to which they had been assigned in view of this emergency. The professor, Washington, Bill, Tom and Andy, who had kept to themselves since the descent, came running out of the small cabin where they usually sat, and wanted to know what it was all about.

"We may hit something, in spite of all precautions," Mr. Henderson remarked. "Slow down the ship."

The Mermaid was, accordingly checked in her downward flight, by a liberal use of the gas and the negative gravity machine.

The bell continued to ring, and the dials pointed to the mark that indicated the ship was more than one hundred and fifty miles down.

Mark, who had run to the engine room to check the descent, came back.

"Why didn't you slow her down?" asked the professor.

"I did," replied the boy. "The negative gravity and the gas machines are working at full speed."

"Then why are we still descending?" asked the scientist. "For a while our speed was checked, but now we are falling faster than before."

"I attended to the apparatus," Mark insisted.

Just then, from without the ship, came a terrible roaring sound, as though there was a great cyclone in progress. At the same time, those aboard the craft could feel themselves being pulled downward with terrific force.

"We are caught in a draught!" Mr. Henderson cried. "We are being sucked down into the depths of the earth!"

He ran to the engine room. With the help of the boys he set in motion an auxiliary gravity machine, designed to exert a most powerful influence against the downward pull of the earth. As they watched the great wheels spin around, and heard the hum and whirr of the dynamos, the boys watched the pointer which indicated how low they were getting.

And, as they watched, they saw that the needle of the dial kept moving, moving, moving.

"Our efforts are useless! We can't stop!" the professor cried.

Grave indeed was the plight of the adventurers. In their ship they were being sucked down into unknown regions and all their efforts did not avail to save them. It was an emergency they could not guard against, and which could not have been foreseen.

"What are to do?" asked Mark.

"We can only wait," Mr. Henderson replied. "The terrible suction may cease, or it may carry us to some place of safety. Let us hope for the best."

Seeing there was no further use in running the engines in an effort to check the downward rush the machines were stopped. Then they waited for whatever might happen.

Now that they seemed in imminent peril Washington was as cool as any one. He went about putting his kitchen in order and getting ready for the next meal as if they were sailing comfortably along on the surface of the ocean. As for old Andy he was nervous and frightened, and plainly showed it. With his gun in readiness he paced back and forth as if on the lookout for strange beasts or birds.

Bill and Tom were so alarmed that they were of little use in doing anything, and they were not disturbed in their staterooms where they went when it became known that the ship was unmanageable.

The boys and the professor, while greatly frightened at the unexpected turn of events, decided there was no use in giving way to foolish alarm. They realized they could do nothing but await developments.

At the same time they took every precaution. They piled all the bedding on the floor of the living room, so that the pillows and mattresses might form a sort of pad in case the ship was dashed down on the bottom of the big hole.

"Not that it would save us much," Jack observed with a grim smile, "but somehow it sort of makes your mind easier."

All this while the ship was being sucked down at a swift pace. The pointer of the gage, indicating the depth, kept moving around and soon they were several hundreds of miles below the surface of the earth.

The professor tried, by means of several instruments, to discover in which direction they were headed, and whether they were going straight down or at an angle. But some strange influence seemed to affect the gages and other pieces of apparatus, for the pointers and hands would swing in all directions, at one time indicating that they were going down, and, again, upward.

"There must be a strong current of electricity here," Mr. Henderson said, "or else there is, as many suspect, a powerful magnet at the center of the earth, which we are nearing."

"What will you do if the ship is pulled apart, or falls and is smashed?" asked Mark with much anxiety.

"You take a cheerful view of things," said Jack.

"Well, it's a good thing to prepare for emergencies," Mark added.

"If the ship was to be separated by the magnetic pull, or if it fell on sharp rocks and was split in twain, I am afraid none of us could do anything to save ourselves," the professor answered. "Still, if we were given a little warning of the disaster, I have means at hand whereby we might escape with our lives. But it would be a perilous way of----"

"I reckon yo' all better come out an' have supper," broke in Washington. "Leastways we'll call it supper, though I don't rightly know whether it's night or mornin'. Anyhow I've got a meal ready."

"I don't suppose any of us feel much like eating," observed Mr. Henderson, "but there is no telling when we will have the chance again, so, perhaps, we had better take advantage of it."

For a while they ate in silence, finding that they had better appetites than they at first thought. Old Andy in particular did full justice to the food Washington had prepared.

"I always found it a good plan to eat as much and as often as you can," the hunter remarked. "This is a mighty uncertain world."

"You started to tell us a little while ago, Professor," said Mark, "about a plan you had for saving out lives if worst came to worst, and there was a chance to put it into operation. What is it?"

"I will tell you," the aged inventor said. "It is something about which I have kept silent, as I did not want to frighten any of you. It was my latest invention, and I had only perfected it when we started off on this voyage. Consequently I had no chance to try it. The machine works in theory, but whether it does in practice is another question. That is why I say there is a risk. But we may have to take this risk. I have placed aboard this ship a----"

The professor was interrupted in what he was about to say by a curious tremor that made the whole ship shiver as though it had struck some obstruction. Yet there was no sudden jolt or jar such as would have been occasioned by that.

At the same time Washington, who was out in the kitchen, came running into the dining room, crying:

"We're droppin' into a ragin' fire, Perfesser!"

"What do you mean?" asked Mr. Henderson.

"I jest took a look down through th' hole in th' bottom of the ship!" cried Washington. "It's all flames an' smoke below us!"

"I wonder if it is the end," the professor muttered in a low voice.

Followed by the boys, the inventor hastened to the floor-window. The lights were turned off to enable a better view to be had of what was below them.

Leaning over the glass protected aperture the boys and the professor saw, far, far down, a bright light shining. It was as if they were miles above a whole town of blast furnaces, the stacks of which were belching forth flames and smoke. The rolling clouds of vapor were illuminated by a peculiar greenish light, which, at times, turned to red, blue, purple and yellowish hues.

The effect was weird and beautiful though it was full of terror for the travelers. It seemed as if they were falling into some terrible pit of fire, for the reflection of what they feared were flames, could plainly be seen.

"I wish I'd never come on this terrible voyage!" wailed Washington. "I'd rather freeze to death than be burned up."

"Washington, be quiet!" commanded the professor sternly. "This is no time for foolishness. We must work hard to save our lives, for we are in dire peril.

"Mark, you and Washington, with Jack, start the engines. Turn on every bit of power you can. Fill the gas holder as full as it will hold, and use extra heavy pressure. I will see if I can not work the negative gravity apparatus to better advantage than we did before. We must escape if possible!"

The boys, as was also Washington, were only too glad to have something to do to take their mind off their troubles. All three were much frightened, but Mark and Jack tried not to show it. As for Washington he was almost crying.

Soon the whirr and hum of the machinery in the Mermaid was heard. The craft, which was rushing in some direction, either downward, ahead or backwards within the unknown depths, shivered from the speed of the dynamos and other apparatus. Soon the boys could hear the professor starting the negative gravity engine, and then began a struggle between the forces of nature and those of mankind.

Once more the adventurers anxiously watched the gages and indicators. For a while the ship seemed to be holding out against the terrible influence that was sucking her down. She appeared to hesitate. Then, as the downward force triumphed over the mechanical energy in the craft, she began to settle again, and soon was descending, if that was the direction, as fast as before.

"It is of no use," said the professor with a groan. "I must try our last resort!"

He started from the engine room where Mark and Jack had gone. As he did so, he glanced at a thermometer hanging on the wall near the door.

"Has any one turned on the heat?" he asked.

"It's shut off," replied Mark, looking at the electric stove.

"Then what makes it so hot?" asked the scientist.

He pointed to the little silvery column in the tiny tube of the instrument. It registered close to one hundred degrees, though a few minutes before it had been but sixty. And the starting of the machinery could not account for the rise in temperature, since most of the apparatus was run by electricity and developed little heat save in the immediate proximity. The thermometer was fully ten feet away from any machine.

"It's the fiery furnace that's doing it!" cried Washington. "We're falling into th' terrible pit an' we're goin' t' be roasted alive!"

"It certainly is getting warmer," observed Mark, as he took off his coat. Soon he had to shed his vest, and Jack and the professor followed his example. The others too, also found all superfluous garments a burden, and, in a little while they were going about in scanty attire.

Still the heat increased, until it was almost torture to remain in the engine room. Nor was it much cooler elsewhere. In vain did the professor set a score of big electric fans to whirring. He even placed cakes of ice, from the small ice machine that was carried, in front of the revolving blades, to cool off the air. But the ice was melted almost as soon as it was taken from the apparatus.

"Them flames is gittin' worser!" Washington cried a little later. "We's comin' nearer!"

From the bottom window the professor and the boys looked down. True enough the curious, changing, vari-colored lights seemed brighter. They could almost see the tongues of flame shooting upward in anticipation of what they were soon to devour.

The heat was increasing every minute. The sides of the ship were hot. The heads of the travelers were getting dizzy. They could hardly talk or move about.

"I must save our lives! I must trust to the----" The professor, who was muttering to himself started toward the storeroom. As in a dream Mark watched him. He remembered afterward that he had speculated on what might be the outcome of the mystery the professor threw about the place. "I will have to use it," he heard the scientist say softly.

Just as Mr. Henderson was about to open the door there came a fiercer blast of heat than any that had preceded. At the same instant the conditions in the Mermaid became so fearful that each of the travelers felt himself fainting away.

"Go to-- storeroom-- get cylinder-- get in----" the professor murmured, and then he fell forward in a faint.

CHAPTER XVI
THE NEW LAND

WHAT is it? Tell us!" exclaimed Jack, almost in his last breath, for, a few seconds later he too toppled over senseless. Then Washington went down, while Andy, Bill and Tom succumbed to the terrible heat.

Mark felt his head swimming. His eyes were almost bulging from their sockets. He dimly remembered trying to force himself to go to the storeroom and see what was there. He started toward it with that intention, but fell half way to it.

As he did so he saw something which impressed itself on his mind, half unconscious as he was.

The door of the storeroom suddenly opened, and from it came a giant shape, that seemed to expand until it filled the whole of the apartment where the stricken ones lay. It was like the form of some monster, half human, half beast. Mark shuddered, and then, closing his eyes, he felt himself sinking down into some terrible deep and black pit. A second later the whole ship was jarred as though it had hit something.

How long he and the others remained unconscious Mark did not know. He was the first to revive, and his first sensation was one as though he had slept hard and long, and did not want to get up. He felt very comfortable, although he was lying flat on the floor, with his head jammed against the side of a locker. It was so dark that he could not distinguish his hand held close to his face.

"I wonder if I'm dead, and if all the others are dead too," he thought to himself. "What has happened? Let's see, the last I remember was some horrible shape rushing from the storeroom. I wonder what it could have been? Surely that was not the secret the professor referred to."

Mark shuddered as he recalled the monster that seemed to have grown more terrible as each second passed. Then the boy raised himself up from his prostrate position.

"Well, at any rate, some one has turned off the heat," he murmured. "It's very comfortable in here now. I wish I could strike a light."

He listened intently, to learn if any of the others were moving about. He could hear them breathing, but so faintly as to indicate they were insensible. Mark stretched out his hand and felt that some one was lying close to him, but who of the adventurers it was he could not determine.

"If only the dynamo was working we could have light," he said. "But it seems to have stopped," and, indeed there was a lacking of the familiar purr and hum of the electrical machine. In fact none of the apparatus in the ship was working.

"The storage battery!" exclaimed Mark. "That would give light for a while, if I can only find the switch in the dark."

He began crawling about on his hands and knees. It was so intensely black that he ran into many things and received severe bruises. At last he came to a doorway, and as he did so his hand came in contact with an easy chair. It was the only one aboard, and by that he knew he had passed into the sitting room. He had his general direction now, and knew if he kept straight on he would come to the engine room. There he was familiar enough with the apparatus and levers to be able to turn the electric switch.

Crawling slowly and cautiously, he reached the room where all the engines were. Then he had to feel around the sides to locate the switch. At length he found it. There was a click, a little flash of greenish fire, and the copper conductors came together, and the ship was flooded with the glow from the incandescents.

Mark hurried back to where the others were lying. They were still unconscious, but an uneasy, movement on the part of Jack told that he was coming out of the stupor. Mark got some ammonia and held it beneath his comrade's nose. The strong fumes completed the work that nature had started and Jack opened his eyes.

"Where am I? What has happened? Are any of them dead?" he asked quickly.

"I hope no one is dead," Mark replied. "As to the other question, I can't answer. I don't know whether we are a thousand miles underground, or floating on the ocean, though I'm more inclined to the former theory. But never mind that now.

Help me to bring the others back to their senses. I'll work on the professor and you can begin on Bill or Tom. Washington seems to be all right," for at that moment the colored man opened his eyes, stared about him and then got up.

"I thought I was dead for suah!" he exclaimed.

"Some of the others may be if we don't hurry," said Mark. "Get to work, Wash!"

With the colored man to help them the two boys, by the use of the ammonia, succeeded in reviving Bill, Tom and old Andy. But the professor, probably on account of his advanced age, did not respond so readily to the treatment. The boys were getting quite alarmed, as even some of the diluted ammonia, forced between his lips, did not cause him to open his eyes, or increase his heart action.

"If he should die, and leave us all alone with the ship in this terrible place, what would we do?" asked Jack.

"He's not going to die!" exclaimed Mark. "Here I have another plan. Washington bring that medical electrical battery from the engine room." This was a small machine the professor had brought along for experimental purposes.

Quickly adjusting it, Mark placed the handles in the nerveless fingers of Mr. Henderson. Then he started the current. In about a minute the eyelids of the aged inventor began to quiver, and, in less than five minutes he had been revived sufficiently to enable him to sit up. He passed his hand across his forehead.

"What has happened?" he asked in a faint voice.

"I don't know; none of us knows," Mark answered. "We all lost our senses when it got so hot, and there seemed to be some peculiar vapor in the air. The last I remember was seeing some horrible shape rush from the storeroom, soon after the ship struck. Then I fainted away. When I woke up I managed to turn the lights on, and then I came back here."

"I wonder where we are," the old man murmured. "I must find out. We must take every precaution. Washington, go and look at the gage indicating our depth."

The colored man was gone but a few seconds. When he returned his eyes were bulging in terror.

"What is it?" asked Mr. Henderson, who, thanks to the battery, had almost completely recovered.

"It ain't possible!" gasped Washington. "I'll never believe it!"

"What is it?" asked Mr. Henderson, while the others waited in anxiety for the answer.

"We're five hundred miles down!" declared Washington.

"Five hundred miles!" muttered the inventor. "It does not seem possible, but it must be so. We fell very rapidly and the terrible draught sucked us down with incredible rapidity. But come, we must see what our situation is, and where we are. We are stationary, and are evidently on some solid substance."

They all felt much recovered now, and, as the terrible fright of being consumed in a fiery furnace had passed, they all were in better spirits.

At the suggestion of the professor, the boys and Washington made a tour of the ship. They found, for some unaccountable reason, that nearly all the engines and apparatuses were out of gear. In some the parts had broken, and others were merely stopped, from the failure of some other machine, on which they were dependent.

"I'm afraid this is the end of the Mermaid," said Mark, in a sorrowful tone.

"Nonsense!" replied Jack, who was of a more cheerful nature. "Things are not so bad as they look. The professor can fix everything."

"I'm sure I hope so," Mark went on, not much encouraged, however, by Jack's philosophy. "It would be no joke to have to stay five hundred miles underground the rest of our lives."

"You don't know," retorted Jack. "Don't judge of a country you've never seen. This may be as fine a place as it is on the surface of the earth. I want a chance to see it," and Jack began to whistle a cheerful tune.

They completed the tour of the ship, and found, that, aside from the damage to the machinery, the Mermaid had not sustained any harm. The hull was in good order, though of course they could not tell about the gas holder. It was not possible to see this except by going into the conning tower or out on the small deck, and this they did not venture to do. The connections between the holder and the main ship seemed to be all right, and there was still a small quantity of gas in the big tank, as Mark found on opening a stop-cock.

They went back to the professor and told him what they had observed. He seemed somewhat alarmed, the more so as the experience he had just passed through had weakened him considerably.

"I hope I shall be able to make the repairs," he said. "It is our only hope."

As he spoke he looked up at the electric lights that shone overhead from wall brackets.

"Who is shutting down the power?" he asked.

"There is no power on, Professor," replied Mark. "I am running the lights from the storage battery. But something is the matter, for they are growing dim."

The filaments were now mere dull red wires, and the ship was being shrouded in gloom again.

"The battery is failing!" exclaimed Mr. Henderson. "We shall be left in darkness, and there is no other way to produce light. I ought to have brought some lamps or candles along in case of emergency,"

The next instant the Mermaid became as black as Egypt is popularly supposed to be, and something like an exclamation of terror came from the professor.

For several minutes they all sat there in the blackness and gloom, waiting for they knew not what. Then, suddenly, there sounded throughout the ship, a creaking as of metal sliding along metal. Some big lever creaked, and, a second later the whole place was flooded with light.

"What has happened?" cried the professor, starting to his feet in alarm.

"We are going to be burned up!" exclaimed old Andy.

"It's all right! It's all right!" yelled Washington from the engine room where the boys had left him. "Don't git skeered! I done it! I opened the port holes, by yanking on the lever. Golly, but we's arrived at the new land! Look out, everybody!"

CHAPTER XVII
A STRANGE COUNTRY

THEY all ran to the port holes, which were openings in the side of the ship. They were fitted with thick, double glass, and covered on the outside with steel shutters. These shutters were worked by a single lever from the engine room, so that one person could open or close them in a second or two. Washington, by accident, it appeared later, had slid back the protecting pieces of steel, and the rest followed.

As the adventurers looked from the glass ports they saw that the light which had flooded the ship came from without. They were in the midst of a beautiful glow, which seemed to be diffused about them like rays from a sun.

Only, in place of being a yellow or white light, such as the sun gives off at varying times, the glow was of violet hue. And, as they watched, they saw the light change color, becoming a beautiful red, then blue, and again green.

"Well, this is certainly remarkable!" the professor said. "I wonder what causes that."

"We've arrived! We're here, anyhow!" Washington cried, coming into the room. "See the country!"

Then, for the first time, the travelers, taking their attention from the curious light that was all around them, saw that they had indeed arrived. They were on a vast plain, one, seemingly, boundless in extent, though off to the left there was a range of lofty mountains, while to the right there was the glimmer of what might be a big lake or inland sea.

"See, we are resting on the ground!" exclaimed Jack. He pointed out of the window, and the others, looking close at hand, noted that the Mermaid had settled down in the midst of what seemed to be a field of flowers. Big red and yellow blossoms were all in front, and some grew so tall as to almost be up to the edge of the port.

"I wonder if we can be seeing aright," the professor muttered. "Is this really the interior of the earth; such a beautiful place as this?"

There could be little doubt of it. The ship had descended through the big shaft, had been sucked down by the terrible air current, and had really landed in a strange country.

Of its size, shape and general conditions the adventurers, as yet, could but guess. They could see it was a pleasant place, and one where there might be the means to sustain life. For, as the professor said afterward, he felt that where there were flowers there would be fruits, and where both of these provisions of nature were to be found there would likely be animal life, and even, perhaps, human beings.

But, for the time, they were content to look from the port on the beautiful scene that lay stretched out before them. The ship rested on an even keel and had landed so softly that none of the plates were strained.

"We have plenty of air, at all events," said the professor as he took a deep breath. "I was afraid of that, but it seems there was no need. The air appears to be as good and fresh as that on the surface of the earth, only there is a curious property to it. It makes one feel larger. I imagine it must be thinner than the air of the earth, which is a rather strange thing, since the higher one goes the more rarefied the air becomes, and the lower, the more dense. Still we can not apply natural philosophy to conditions under the earth. All the usual theories may be upset. However, we should be content to take things as we find them, and be glad we were not dashed to pieces when the ship was caught in the terrible current."

"What do you suppose caused the awful heat, and then made it go away again?" asked Jack.

"I can only make a guess at it," Mr. Henderson answered. "There are many strange things we will come across if we stay here long, I believe. As for the fire I think we must have passed a sort of interior volcano."

"But what sort of a place do you think we have come to, Professor?" asked Mark.

"It is hard to say," the scientist replied. "We are certainly somewhere within the earth. Our gage tells us it is five hundred miles. That may or may not be correct, but I believe we are several hundred miles under the crust, at all events. As to what sort of a place it is, you can see for yourselves."

"But how is it we can breathe here, and things can grow?" asked Bill, who was beginning to lose his fright at the thought of being practically buried alive.

"I do not know what makes such things possible," Mr. Henderson replied, "but that there is air here is a certainty. I can hardly believe it is drawn from the surface of the earth, down the big hole, and I am inclined to think this place of the under-world has an atmosphere of its own, and one which produces different effects than does our own."

"They certainly have larger flowers than we have," said Mark. "See how big they grow, and what strong colors they have."

He pointed to the port, against which some of the blooms were nodding in the wind that had sprung up, for, in spite of the many differences, the under-world was in some respects like the upper one.

"Probably the difference in the atmosphere accounts for that," the professor said. "It enables things to grow larger. And, by the way, Mark, that reminds me of something you said about seeing some horrible monster fleeing from the ship. Did you dream that?"

"I did see something horrible, Professor," he answered. "I'm not positive what it was, but I'll tell you as nearly as I can what it was like."

Thereupon Mark detailed what he had seen.

"But how could anything, least of all some big monster, be concealed in the storeroom, and we not know anything about it?" asked Mr. Henderson.

"I thought you did know something of it," replied Mark.

"Who, me? My dear boy, you must be dreaming again. Why should I want to conceal any being in the storeroom? Come, there is something back of this. Tell me all you know of it. I can't imagine why you think I was hiding something in the apartment."

"I thought so because you were always so anxious not to have me go near it," answered the boy. "Don't you remember when you saw me going toward it, several times, you warned me away?"

"So I did!" exclaimed Mr. Henderson, a light breaking over his face. "But, Mark, it was not because I had hidden some human being or animal there. I can't tell you what it is yet, save that I can say it is merely a machine of mine that I have invented. For reasons of my own I don't want any one to see it yet. Perhaps it may never be seen. I thought, not long ago, that we might have to undertake a terrible risk in escaping from this place. I directed you to go to the storeroom-- but there, I can't say any more, my friends. Sufficient that I had nothing in the animal line concealed there."

"But I am certain there was some beast or human being in there," insisted Mark. "I heard curious noises in there. Besides, how do you account for the food disappearing and the door being open at times?"

"It might have been rats," said Jack.

"I don't believe there are rats in the ship," put in the professor. "More likely it was one of us who got up hungry and took the victuals."

"I'm sorry I can't agree with you," Mark added respectfully. "I am sure some strange being was on board this ship, and I believe it has now escaped. Who or what it was I can't say, but you'll find I'm right, some day."

"All right," spoke Mr. Henderson with a laugh. "I like to see any one brave enough to stick up for his opinion, but, at the same time, I can't very well imagine any person or thing being concealed in that storeroom ever since we started. How could it get in?"

Mark did not; answer, but there came to him the recollection of that night, previous to the sailing of the Flying Mermaid, when he had observed some strange shadow that seemed to glide aboard the craft.

"Now let's forget all about such things," the professor went on. "We are in a strange country, and there are many things to see and do. Let's explore a little. Then we must see what we can do with the ship. We are dependent on it, and it will not do to allow it to remain in a damaged state. We expect to travel many miles in the interior of the earth if it is possible, and we have only our craft to go in."

"I reckon we'd all better assimilate into our interior progression some molecules and atoms of partly disentegrated matter in order to supply combustion for the carbonaceous elements and assist in the manufacture of red corpuscles," said Washington, appearing in the door, with a broad grin on his good-natured face.

"Which, being interpreted," the professor said, "means, I suppose, that we had better eat something to keep our digestive apparatus in good working order?"

"Yo' done guessed it!" exclaimed the colored man, relapsing into his ordinary speech. "I'se got a meal all ready."

They agreed that they might not have another opportunity soon to partake of food, so they all gathered about the table, on which Washington had spread a good meal.

"Come on, let's go outside and view this new and strange land at closer quarters," the professor said, when they had satisfied their appetites. "We can't see much from inside the ship."

Accordingly the heavy door in the side of the Mermaid was slid back, and, for the first time the travelers stepped out on the surface of the land in the interior of the earth.

At first it seemed no different than the ordinary land to which they were accustomed. But they soon found it had many strange attributes. The queer shifting and changing light, with the myriad of hues was one of them, but to this the adventurers had, by this time, become accustomed, though it was, none the less, a marvel to them. It was odd enough to see the landscape blood red one instant, and a pale green the next, as it does when you look through differently colored glasses.

Then, too, they noticed that the grass and flowers grew much more abundantly than in the outer part of the world. They saw clover six feet high, and blades of grass even taller. In some places the growth of grass was so big that they were in danger of getting lost in it.

"If the grass is like this, what will the trees be?" asked Mark.

"There are some away over there," Jack replied. "We'll have to take a sail over. They must be several hundred feet high."

"Well, at any rate, here's a little brook, and the water looks good to drink," went on Mark. "I'm thirsty, so here goes."

He hurried to where a stream was flowing sluggishly between grassy banks. The water was as clear as crystal, and Mark got down on his face and prepared to sip some of the liquid up.

But, no sooner had his lips touched it, than he sprang up with a cry and stood gazing at the water.

"What's the matter?" asked Jack. "Hot?"

"No, it isn't hot," Mark replied, "but it isn't water. It's white molasses!"

"White molasses?" repeated the professor, coming up at that moment. "What are you talking about?"

He stooped down and dipped his finger into the stream. He drew it up quickly, and there ran from it big drops that flowed as slowly as the extract of the sugarcane does in cold weather.

"You're about right, Mark," he said. "It's water but it's almost as thick as molasses." He touched his finger to his tongue. "It's good to drink, all right," he went on, "only it will be a little slow going down."

Then he dipped up a palm full, and let it trickle down his throat.

"It is the strangest water I ever saw," he added. "It must be that the lack of some peculiar property of air, which we have on the surface, has caused this. I must make some notes on it," and he drew out pencil and paper. He was about to jot down some facts when he was interrupted by a cry from Washington.

"Come and see what's the matter with this stone!" he cried.

CHAPTER XVIII
CAUGHT BY A STRANGE PLANT

WASHINGTON is in trouble!" exclaimed Mr. Henderson. Followed by the two boys he ran to where the colored man stood in a stooping position over a small pile of stones.

"What is it? Has something bit you?" asked the scientist, as he came up on the run.

"No, but I can't git this stone up!" Washington said. "Look at what a little stone it is, but I can't lift it. Something must have happened to me. Maybe some one put th' evil eye on me! Maybe I'm bewitched!"

"Nonsense!" exclaimed the professor, "what did you want the stone for?"

"Nothin' in particular," replied Washington, still tugging away at the stone, which was the size of his head. "I was just goin' t' throw it at a big bird, but when I went to lift it this little stone 'peared t' be glued fast."

Washington moved aside to give Mr. Henderson a chance to try to pick up the piece of rock. As the scientist grasped it a look of surprise came over his features:

"This is most remarkable!" he exclaimed. "I can't budge it. I wonder if a giant magnet is holding it down."

He tugged and tugged until he was red in the face. Then he beckoned to the two boys, and they came to his aid. There was barely room for them all to each get one hand on the rock, and then, only after a powerful tug did it come up. Almost instantly it dropped back to the earth.

"This is remarkable!" the professor said. "I wonder if the other stones are the same."

He tried several others, and one and all resisted his efforts. It was only the small stones he was able to lift alone, and these, he said, were so weighty that it would have been a task to throw them any distance.

"The water and the stones are strangely heavy in this land," he said. "I wonder what other queer things we shall see."

"I saw a bird a little while ago, when I went to pick up that stone," observed Washington.

"What kind was it?" asked the inventor.

"I don't know, only it was about as big as an eagle."

The travelers wandered about a quarter of a mile from the ship. They avoided the tall grass and the lofty nodding flowers that seemed to grow in regular groves, and kept to places where they could walk with comparative freedom.

"Have you formed any idea, Professor, as to the nature of this country?" asked Mark, who liked to get at the bottom of things.

"I have, but it is only a theory," Mr. Henderson answered. "I believe we are on a sort of small earth that is inside the larger one we live on. This sphere floats in space, just as our earth does, and we have passed through the void that lies between our globe and this interior one. I think this new earth is about a quarter the size of ours and in some respects the same. In others it is vastly different.

"But we will not think of those things now. We must see what our situation is, whether we are in any danger, and must look to repairing our ship. There will be time enough for other matters later."

The travelers were walking slowly along, noting the strange things on every side. As they advanced the vegetation seemed to become more luxuriant, as if nature had tried to out-do herself in providing beautiful flowers and plants. The changing lights added to the beauty and weirdness of the scene.

The plain was a rolling one, and here and there were small hills and hollows. As the travelers topped a rise Jack, who was in advance, called out:

"Oh what queer plants! They are giant Jacks-in-the-pulpit!"

The others hastened forward to see what the boy had discovered. Jack was too eager to wait, and pressed on. The hill which sloped away from the top of the little plateau on which he stood, was steeper than he had counted on. As he leaned forward he lost his balance and toppled, head foremost, down the declivity, rolling over.

"Look out!" cried Mark, who had almost reached his comrade's side.

The scene that confronted the travelers was a strange one. Before them in a sort of hollow, were scores of big plants, shaped somewhat like a Jack-in-the-pulpit, or a big lily, with a curved top or flap to it.

The plants were about eight feet tall, three feet across the top, and the flap or covering was raised about two feet. They were nodding and swaying in the wind on their short stems.

"He's headed right for one of them!" Mr. Henderson exclaimed. "I hope he'll not fall into one of the openings."

"Is there any danger?" asked Mark.

"I'm afraid there is," the inventor added. "Those plants are a variety of the well-known pitcher plant, or fly-trap, as they are sometimes called. In tropical countries they grow to a large size, but nothing like these. They are filled, in the cup, with a sort of sticky, sweet mixture, and this attracts insects. When one enters the cup the top flap folds over, and the hapless insect is caught there. The plant actually devours it, nature providing a sort of vegetable digestive apparatus. These giant plants are the same, and they seem large enough to take in a man, to say nothing of Jack!"

With anxious faces the adventurers turned to watch the fate of their comrade. Jack was slipping, sliding and rolling down the hill. He could not seem to stop, though he was making desperate efforts to do so. He was headed straight for one of the largest of the terrible plants.

In vain, as he saw what was in front of him, did he try to change the course of his involuntary voyage. Over and over he rolled, until, at length, he struck a little grassy hummock, bounced into the air, and right into the opening of a monster pitcher plant.

"It has him!" cried Mark. "We must save him! Come on everyone!"

He raced down the hill, while the others came closely after him. They reached the plant into which Jack had bounced. The flap, or top piece, had closed down, tightly over the unfortunate boy.

"Quick! We must save him or he will be smothered to death or drowned in the liquid the cup contains!" Mr. Henderson exclaimed. "Attack the plant with any-thing you can find!"

"Let's cut through the side of the flower-cup!" suggested Mark. "That seems softer than the stem."

His idea was quickly put into operation. Andy's long hunting knife came in very handy. While the sides of the long natural cup were tough, the knife made an impression on them, and, soon, a small door or opening had been cut in the side of the pitcher plant, large enough to enable a human body to pass through.

When the last fibre had been severed by Andy, who was chosen to wield the knife because of his long practice as a hunter, there was a sudden commotion within the plant. Then a dark object, dripping water, made a spring and landed almost at the feet of the professor.

It was Jack, and a sorry sight he presented. He was covered from head to foot with some sticky substance, which dripped from all over him.

With hasty movements he cleared the stuff from his eyes and mouth, and spluttered:

"It's a good thing you cut me out when you did. I couldn't have held on much longer!"

CHAPTER XIX
THE BIG PEACH

JACK soon recovered from his remarkable experience. The terrible plant that had nearly eaten him alive was a mass of cut-up vegetable matter which attracted a swarm of insects. Most of them were ants, but such large ones the boys had never seen before, and the professor said they exceeded in size anything he had read about. Some of them were as large as big rats. They bit off large pieces of the fallen plant and carried them to holes in the ground which were big enough for Washington to slip his foot into, and he wore a No. 11 shoe.

But the adventurers felt there were more important things for them to look at than ants, so they started away again, the professor telling them all to be careful and avoid accidents.

It was while they were strolling through a little glade, which they came upon unexpectedly, that Washington, who was in the lead called out:

"Gracious goodness! It must be Thanksgivin'!"

"Why so?" asked Jack.

"'Cause here's th' remarkablest extraordinary and expansionist of a pumpkin that ever I laid eyes on!" the colored man cried.

They all hurried to where Washington had come to a halt. There, on the ground in front of him, was a big round object, about the size of a hogshead. It was yellow in color, and was not unlike the golden vegetable from which mothers make such delicious pies.

"I allers was fond of pumpkins," said Washington, placing his hand on the thing, which was almost as tall as he was, "but I never thought I'd come across such a one as this."

The professor and the two boys went closer to the monstrosity. Mr. Henderson passed his hand over it and then, bending closer, smelled of it.

"That's not a pumpkin!" he exclaimed.

"What is it then?" asked Washington.

"It's a giant peach," the inventor remarked. "Can't you see the fuzz, and smell it? Of course it's a peach."

"Well I'll be horn-swoggled!" cried Washington, leaning against the big fruit, which easily, supported him.

"Hurrah!" cried Jack, drawing his knife from his pocket and opening the largest blade. "I always did like peaches. Now I can have all I want," and he drove the steel into the object, cutting off a big slice which he began to eat.

"It may be poisonous!" exclaimed Mark.

"Too late now," responded Jack, the juice running down from his mouth. "Taste's good, anyhow."

They all watched Jack while he devoured his slice of fruit. Washington acted as if he expected his friend to topple over unconscious, but Jack showed no bad symptoms.

"You'd better all have some," the boy said. "It's the best I ever tasted."

Encouraged by Jack's example, Mark thought he, too, would have some of the fruit. He opened his knife and was about to take off some of the peach when suddenly the thing began to roll forward, almost upon him.

"Hi! Stop your shoving!" he exclaimed. "Do you want to have the thing roll over me, Jack?"

"I'm not shoving!" replied Jack.

"Some one is!" Mark went on. He dodged around the far side of the immense fruit and what he saw made him cry out in astonishment.

Two grasshoppers, each one standing about three feet high, were standing on their hind legs, and with their fore feet were pushing the peach along the ground. They had been attracted to the fruit by some juice which escaped from a bruise on that side, which was the ripest, and, being fond of sweets had, evidently decided to take their find to some safe place where they could eat it at their leisure. Or perhaps they wanted to provide for their families if grasshoppers have them.

"Did you ever see such monsters?" asked Jack. "They're as big as dogs!"

At the sound of his voice the two grasshoppers, becoming alarmed, ceased their endeavors to roll the peach along, and, assuming a crouching attitude seemed to be waiting.

"They certainly are remarkable specimens," Mr. Henderson said. "If the other animals are in proportion, and if there are persons in this new world, we are likely to have a hard time of it."

This time the immense insects concluded the strangers were not to their liking. With a snapping of their big muscular legs and a whirr of their wings that was like the starting of an automobile, the grasshoppers rose into the air and sailed away over the heads of the adventurers. Their flight was more than an eighth of a mile in extent, and they came down in a patch of the very tall grass.

"Let's go after them!" exclaimed old Andy. "I was so excited I forgot to take a shot at them. Come on!"

"I think we'd better not," counseled the professor. "In the first place we don't need them. They would be no good for food. Then we don't know but what they might attack us, and it would be no joke to be bitten by a grasshopper of that size. Let them alone. We may find other game which will need your attention, Andy. Better save your ammunition."

Somewhat against his will, Andy had to submit to the professor's ruling. The old hunter consoled himself with the reflection that if insects grew to that size he would have some excellent sport hunting even the birds of the inner world.

"I wonder what sort of a tree that peach grew on," Jack remarked, as he cut off another slice, when the excitement caused by the discovery of the grasshoppers had subsided. "It must be taller than a church steeple. I wonder how the fruit got here, for there are no trees around."

"I fancy those insects rolled it along for a good distance," Mr. Henderson put in. "You can see the marks on the ground, where they pushed it. They are wonderful creatures."

"Are we going any farther?" asked Mark. "Perhaps we can find the peach tree, and, likely there are other fruit trees near it."

At the professor's suggestion they strolled along for some distance. They were now about three miles from the airship, and found that what they had supposed was a rather level plain, was becoming a succession of hills and hollows. It was while descending into a rather deep valley that Jack pointed ahead and exclaimed:

"I guess there's our peach orchard, but I never saw one like it before."

Nor had any of the others. Instead of trees the peaches were attached to vines growing along the ground. They covered a large part of the valley, and the peaches, some bigger than the one they first discovered, some small and green, rose up amid the vines, just as pumpkins do in a corn field.

"Stranger and stranger," the professor murmured. "Peaches grow on vines. I suppose potatoes will grow on trees. Everything seems to be reversed here."

They made their way down toward the peach "orchard" as Jack called it, though "patch" would have been a better name. Besides peaches they found plums, apples, and pears growing in the same way, and all of a size proportionate to the first-named fruit.

"Well, one thing is evident," Mr. Henderson remarked, "we shall not starve here. There is plenty to eat, even if we have to turn vegetarians."

"I wonder what time it is getting to be," Jack remarked. "My watch says twelve o'clock but whether it's noon or midnight I can't tell, with this colored light coming and going. I wonder if it ever sets as the sun does."

"That is something we'll have to get used to," the professor said. "But I think we had better go back to the ship now. We have many things to do to get it in order again. Besides, I am a little afraid to leave it unguarded so long. No telling but what some strange beast-- or persons, for that matter-- might injure it."

"I'm going to take back some slices of peaches with me, anyhow," Mark said, and he and Jack cut off enough to make several meals, while Bill, Tom and Washington took along all they could carry.

As they walked back toward the ship the strange lights seemed to be dying out. At first they hardly noticed this, but as they continued on it became quite gloomy, and an odd sort of gloom it was too, first green, then yellow, then red and then blue.

"I believe whatever serves as a sun down here is setting," the professor observed. "We must hurry. I don't want to be caught out here after dark."

They hurried on, the lights dying out more and more, until, as they came in sight of their ship, it was so black they could hardly see.

Mark who was in the rear turned around, glancing behind him. As he did so he caught sight of a gigantic shadow moving along on top of the nearest hill. The shadow was not unlike that of a man in shape, but of such gigantic stature that Mark knew it could be like no human being he had ever seen. At the same time it bore a curious resemblance to the weird shadow he had seen slip into the Mermaid that night before they sailed.

"I wonder if it can be the same-- the same thing-- grown larger, just as the peach grows larger than those in our world," Mark thought, while a shiver of fear seemed to go over him. "I wonder if that-- that thing could have been on the ship----"

Then the last rays of light died away and there was total darkness.

CHAPTER XX
OVERHAULING THE SHIP

KEEP together!" shouted the professor. "It will not do to become lost now. We are close to the ship, and will soon be there. Come after me."

It was more by following the sound of the scientist's voice, than by any sight which the others could get of him, that they managed to trail along behind. They reached the ship in safety, however, and entered. There was no sound as of beasts or insects within, and, though Mark felt a little apprehensive on account of what he had seen, he and the others as well, were glad to be again in something that seemed like home.

"I wish we had some candles, or some sort of a light to see by," the professor remarked. "We can do nothing in the dark, and there is no telling how long this night is going to last once it has set in. If I could have a little illumination, I might be able to fix the dynamo, and then we could turn on the incandescents. That portable light we had is broken."

"By cracky!" exclaimed Andy. "I believe I have the very thing!"

"You don't mean to say you have a torch or a candle with you, do you?" asked Mr. Henderson.

"No, but I have my patent pipe lighting apparatus," the hunter said. "I always carry it. It gives a little light, but not much, though it may be enough to work by."

Not until after several hours work, handicapped as they were by lack of light, were the repairs to the ship completed.

"Now we'll start the engine and see how we will come out," the inventor exclaimed, as he wiped his hands on some waste.

It did not take long to generate enough power to turn the dynamo. Soon the familiar hum and whirr was heard, and, a few seconds later the filaments in the lamps began to glow a dull red, which gradually brightened until they were shining in all their usual brilliancy.

"Hurrah!" cried the boys. "Now we can see!"

They all felt in better spirits with the restoration of the lights, and, washing off the grease and dirt of their labors in the engine room, they prepared to sit down to the meal which Washington prepared.

As soon as the dynamo was working well, care had to be taken not to speed it too much on account of a mended belt. The professor turned off part of the lights and switched some of the current into the storage batteries, to provide for emergencies. For there was no telling how long the night might last.

Jack was the first one to finish the meal-- they did not know whether to call it dinner, supper or breakfast. He went into the conning tower, and, as soon as he reached it he called out:

"Come on up here, professor! There's something strange going on!"

Mr. Henderson, followed by Mark, hurried to the tower. As he reached it and looked out of the forward window, a beautiful white glow illuminated the whole scene, and then, from below the horizon, there arose seven luminous disks. One was in the centre, while about it circled the other six, like some immense pin-wheel.

"It's the moon!" cried Mark.

"It's seven moons!" Jack exclaimed. "Why it's almost as light as day!"

And so it was, for the seven moons, if that is what they were, gave an illumination not unlike the sun in brilliancy though it was like the beams from the pale moon of the earth.

"I guess we need not have worried about the darkness," the professor remarked. "Still it is a good thing I fixed the dynamo."

For some time he and the other adventurers watched the odd sight of the moons, as they rose higher and higher overhead. The scene was a beautiful, if weird one, for the whole plain was bathed in the soft light.

"I guess we can turn off the incandescents, and use all the power for the storage batteries," Mr. Henderson went on, as he descended into the ship, and opened the port shutters which had been closed when they started off on their exploring tour. The interior of the Mermaid was almost as light as when the odd colored beams had been playing over the new earth to which they had come.

"I think we had better continue with our work of making repairs," Mr. Henderson said. "We can't count on these moons remaining here any length of time, and I want to take advantage of them. So though some of us perhaps need sleep, we will forego it and fix up the Mermaid. I want to take a trip and see what other wonders await us."

They all agreed that they would rather work than sleep, and soon the entire force was busy in the engine room. There was much to be done, and the most important things were attended to first. The motive power was overhauled and found to be in need of several new parts. These were put in and then the gas generator, and the negative gravity machine, were put in shape.

It would have taken something very substantial to have awakened any one on board the Mermaid that night. They all slept soundly and awoke to find the strange colored lights shining in through the glass covered port holes.

"Well, the sun, or what corresponds to it, is up," observed Jack, "and I guess we had better do as the little boy in the school reader did, and get up, too, Mark."

Soon all the travelers were aroused, and the sound of Washington bustling about in the kitchen, whence came the smell of coffee, bacon and eggs, told the hungry ones that breakfast was under way.

After the meal work was again started on repairing the ship, and by noon the professor remarked:

"I think we shall try a little flight after dinner. That is, if one thing doesn't prevent us."

"What is that?" asked Jack.

"We may be held down, as were those stones," was the grave answer.

CHAPTER XXI
THE FISH THAT WALKED

IT was with no little apprehension that the professor prepared to take his first flight aboard the ship in the realms of the new world. He knew little or nothing of the conditions he might meet with, the density of the atmosphere, or how the Mermaid would behave under another environment than that to which she was accustomed.

Yet he felt it was necessary to make a start. They would have to attempt a flight sooner or later, and Mr. Henderson was not the one to delay matters. So, the last adjustment having been made to the repaired machinery, they all took their places in the ship.

The boys and the professor went to the conning tower to direct matters, while Washington and the others were in the engine room to see that the machinery worked properly. Mark gave a last look outside as he closed the big steel cover over the hole through which admission was had to the craft. He thought he might catch a glimpse of the queer shadow, but nothing was in sight. It was like a beautiful summer's day, save for the strange lights, shifting and changing. But the travelers had become somewhat used to them by this time.

The professor turned the valve that allowed the gas to enter the holder. There was a hissing sound and a sort of trembling throughout the entire ship. The dynamos were whizzing away and the negative gravity machine was all ready to start.

For several minutes the travelers waited until the big lifting tank was filled with the strong vapor. They watched the gages which indicated the pressure to be several hundred pounds.

"I think we can chance it now," remarked Mr. Henderson, as he threw over several levers. "We'll try, at any rate."

With a tremor the Mermaid left the surface of the inner earth and went sailing upward toward the-- well it wasn't exactly the sky, but it was what corresponded to it in the new world, though there were no clouds and no blue depths such as the boys were used to. At all events the Mermaid was flying again, and, as the adventurers felt themselves being lifted up they gave a spontaneous cheer at the success which had crowned their efforts.

The ship went up several hundred feet, and then, the professor, having brought her to a stop, sent her ahead at a slow pace. He wanted to be sure all the apparatus was in good working order before he tried any speed.

The Mermaid responded readily. Straight as an arrow through the air she flew.

"Well, this is almost as good as being on the regular earth!" exclaimed Jack.

"It's better," put in Mark. "We haven't seen half the wonders yet. Let's open the floor shutter, and see how it looks down below."

He and Jack went to the room where there was an opening in the floor of the ship, covered by heavy glass. They slid back the steel shutter and there, down below them, was the strange new, world they had come to, stretched out like some big map.

They could see mountains, forests, plains, and rivers, the water sparkling in the colored light. Over green fields they flew, then across some stretches where only sand and rocks were to be seen. Faster and faster the ship went, as the professor found the machinery was once more in perfect order. Jack was idly watching the play of tinted lights over the surface of the ground.

"I wonder what makes it," he said.

"I have tried to account for it in several ways," said the professor, who had called Washington to the conning tower and come to join the boys. "I have had first one theory and then another, but the one I am almost sure is correct is that hidden volcanic fires cause the illumination.

"I think they flare up and die away, and have become so regular that they produce the same effect as night and day with us. Probably the fires go out for lack of fuel, and when it is supplied they start up again. Perhaps it is a sort of gas that they burn."

"Well, it's queer enough, whatever it is," Jack remarked. "What strikes me as funny, though, is that we haven't seen a single person since we came here. Surely this place must be inhabited."

Mark thought of the strange shadow he had seen, but said nothing.

"I believe it is," the professor answered. "We will probably come upon the inhabitants soon. I only hope they are a people who will do us no harm."

"If they tried any of their tricks we could mount up in our ship and escape them," said Andy.

"Provided they gave us the chance," Mr. Henderson put in. "Well, we'll not worry about that now."

For several hours the ship traveled on, until it had come to a different sort of country. It was wilder and not so level, and there were a number of streams and small lakes to be seen.

"Are you going to sail all night?" asked Jack.

"No," replied the professor. "I think we'll descend very soon now, and camp out for a while. That lake just ahead seems to offer a good place," and he pointed to a large sheet of water that sparkled in the distance, for by this time they had all gone back to the conning tower.

The lake was in the midst of a wood that extended for some distance on all sides, and was down in a sort of valley. The ship headed toward it, and in a short time a landing was made close to shore.

"Maybe we can have some fresh fish for supper," exclaimed Jack as he ran from the ship as soon as the sliding door in the side was opened. "Looks as if that lake had some in it. It is not thick water like in that stream we stopped at," he added.

"I believe you're right," old Andy put in, as he turned back to look for some lines and hooks among his traps. He soon found what he wanted, and gave them to the boys, taking his trusty gun along for himself.

While the professor, Washington, Tom and Bill remained behind to make some adjustments to the machinery, and to get things in shape for the night, which, they calculated would soon be upon them, Jack, Mark and Andy went down to the shore of the lake. The boys cut some poles from the trees, and baiting the hooks with some fat worms found under the bark, threw in.

"Let's see who'll get the first bite," spoke Jack. "I'm pretty generally lucky at fishing."

"Well, while you're waiting to decide that there contest, I think I'll take a stroll along shore and see if I can see anything to shoot," Andy remarked.

For several minutes the boys sat in silence on the bank of the lake, watching the play of the vari-colored lights on the water. Suddenly Jack felt a quiver on his line, and his pole began to shake.

"I've got something!" he cried. Then his pole bent almost double and he began to pull for all he was worth. "It's a whopper!" he cried. "Come and help me, Mark!"

Mark ran to his friend's aid. Whatever was on the other end of the line was strong enough to tax the muscles of both boys. They could hear the pole beginning to break. But for the excellent quality of Andy's line that would have parted some time before.

All at once there came a sudden slacking of the pull from whatever was in the water. And so quickly did it cease that both boys went over backward in a heap.

"He's got away!" cried Jack, getting up and brushing some of the dirt from his clothes.

"There's something that didn't get away!" cried Mark, who had risen to his knees, and was pointing at the lake. Jack looked and what he saw made him almost believe he was dreaming.

For, emerging from the water, dragging the pole and line the boys had dropped along with it, was a most curious creature. It was a big fish, but a fish with four short legs on which it was walking, or rather waddling along as much as a duck, with a double supply of feet, might do.

"Say, do I see that or is there something the matter with my eyes?" sung out Jack, making ready to run away.

"It's there all right!" exclaimed Mark. "Hi! Andy! Here's something to shoot!" he yelled, for indeed the creature was big enough to warrant attack with a gun. It was about five feet long and two feet through.

On and on it came, straight at the boys, as if to have revenge for the pain the fish hook must have caused it, for the barb could be seen dangling from its lip. On and on it came, waddling forward, the water dripping from it at every step. It had the body and general shape of a fish, save that the tail was rather large in proportion. As it came nearer the boys noted that the feet were webbed, like those of a water fowl.

"Come on!" cried Jack. "It may attack us!"

At that moment the creature opened its mouth, showing a triple row of formidable teeth, and gave utterance to a sort of groan and grunt combined.

This was enough to send Jack and Mark off on a run up the bank, and did they stop until they heard Andy's voice hailing them.

"What's the matter, boys?"

"Come here! Quick!" answered Jack.

The fish-animal had halted and seemed to be taking an observation. To do this, as it could not turn its neck, it had to shift its whole body. Old Andy came up on the run, his gun held in readiness.

"Where is it?" he asked, and the boys pointed silently.

The hunter could not repress a start of astonishment as he saw the strange creature. But he did not hesitate a second. There was a crack of the rifle, and the thing, whatever it was, toppled over, dead.

Andy hurried up to it, to get a closer view.

"Well, this is the limit!" he exclaimed. "First we have grasshoppers that can roll peaches as big as hogsheads, and now we come across fish that walk. I wonder what we will see next."

"I don't want to go fishing in this lake any more," spoke Jack, as he looked at the repulsive creature. "I never want to eat fish any more."

"Same here," agreed Mark, and old Andy was of the opinion that the thing killed would not make a wholesome dish for the table.

"There don't seem to be any game in this section," he remarked. "Not a sign could I see, nor have I since we have been here, unless you count those grasshoppers. But the fruit is good, I'll say that."

"Come on, we'd better be getting back," Mark said, as he noticed it was getting dark. "I'm hungry."

CHAPTER XXII
THE SNAKE-TREE

THEY managed to make a good meal of the food supplies they had brought along, and as a dessert Washington made some peach short-cake from the slices of the giant fruit they had found, the day before. Just as they finished supper it got very dark, but, in about an hour, the moon-beams, as the travelers called them, came up, and illuminated the lake with a weird light.

As the machinery of the Mermaid was now in working order there was no further alarm because of the darkness. The ship rested on a level keel about a hundred yards back from the lake, and, seeing that all was snug, and the fastenings secure, the travelers went to bed.

Though they had to forego fish for breakfast the travelers made a good meal. After seeing that the ship was in readiness for a quick start, the professor suggested they take a walk around and see what sort of country they might be in now.

They tramped on for several miles, meeting with no adventures, and seeing nothing out of the ordinary. It was a pleasant day, just warm enough to be comfortable, and a little wind was blowing through the trees.

"It would be almost like home if it wasn't for the strange lights, and the memory of the queer things here," said Jack. "I feel fine. Let's see if you can hit that dead tree over there, Mark."

Jack stooped to grab up a stone, but no sooner had his fingers touched it than he called out:

"There! I forgot all about the stones here being heavier than lead. Guess we can't throw any of 'em. But come on. I'll race you to the dead tree!"

Mark was willing, so the two boys set off at a fast pace.

"Look out where you're going!" the professor called after them. "No telling what may be in those woods," for the boys were approaching a little glade, on the edge of which the dead tree stood.

Jack reached the goal first, and stood leaning against the trunk, waiting for Mark.

"You'd better practice sprinting!" exclaimed the victor.

Mark was about to excuse himself for his poor showing, on the plea of having eaten too much breakfast, when to his horror he saw what seemed to be a long thin snake spring out from the branches of a nearby tree and twine itself about Jack.

"Help me! Save me!" cried the unfortunate boy, as he was lifted high into the air and pulled within the shadow of the wood.

For an instant Mark was too horror-stricken to move. Then with a shout that alarmed the others, who were coming along more slowly, he made a dash for the place he had last seen Jack.

Had old Andy not been on the watch, with those keen eyes of his, there might have been a double tragedy. He had seen from afar the sudden snatching up of Jack, and noted Mark's rush to save his chum.

"Stand still! Don't go in there for your life!" yelled the hunter, at the same time running forward with gun ready.

His example was followed by the professor, Washington and the other two men.

"A snake has Jack!" called Mark, when Andy was at his side.

"No! It's not a snake!" replied the hunter. "It's worse. It's the snake-tree!"

"What's that?" asked Mr. Henderson, hurrying up.

"The snake-tree has Jack," the hunter went on. "It is a plant, half animal, half-vegetable. It has long branches, not unlike a snake in shape. They can move about and grab things."

"One of them got a grip on Jack as he leaned against the dead tree trunk. I just caught a glimpse of it, and called to prevent Mark from running into danger."

"Can't we save him?" asked Mr. Henderson.

"I'm going to try!" replied Andy. "Quick! Gather up some pieces of dry wood. I have some paper, and my pipe lighter. We must fight the snake-tree with fire!"

CHAPTER XXIII
THE DESERTED VILLAGE

JACK'S Cries were growing fainter and fainter. Peering in through the branches of the dead tree the professor could see the whip-like limbs winding closer and closer about the boy.

"I am afraid we will be too late!" he said.

Andy had twisted some paper into a rude torch. He set fire to it with his pocket lighter, and, when Bill and Mark brought him some little pieces of dead wood the old hunter added them to his bundle, which was now blazing brightly.

"How are you going to do it?" asked the professor.

"I'll show you," replied Andy. He bound the sticks and paper together with wisps of grass and then, when it was so hot he could hardly hold it longer, he ran as close as he dared to the snake-tree and tossed the torch at the foot of it.

The blazing bundle fell among some damp leaves and grass, as Andy had intended it should, and soon a dense smoke arose, pouring straight up through the branches of the animal-tree, the limbs of which were gathered in a knot about the half-unconscious form of the boy.

For a few minutes they all waited anxiously. Would Andy's trick succeed? Had the terrible tree not already squeezed the life from Jack?

But, while they watched, there seemed to come a change over the tree. The snake-like arms waved less and less. They seemed to straighten out, as though deprived of power by the smoke which was now so dense as to hide Jack from sight. Then the arms suddenly relaxed and something rolled from them and fell to the ground. With a quick movement Andy darted in, crawling on his hands and knees beneath the limbs, and brought Jack out. The boy was white and his eyes were closed.

"Get some water!" cried the old hunter.

Mark ran toward a stream a little distance away. He brought some of the curiously thick liquid in his hat, and while Andy held the boy the professor sprinkled some of the drops on his face, and forced some between his lips. In a little while Jack's eyes slowly opened.

"Don't let it eat me!" he begged.

"You're all right now," said Andy heartily. "Not a bit harmed, Jack. But," he added in a low tone, "it was a close call."

A few whiffs from a bottle of ammonia the professor carried soon brought Jack's color back.

"Do you feel better now?" asked Mark.

"I guess so. Yes, I'm all right," replied Jack, struggling to his feet. "What happened? Feels as if I had been tied up with a lot of rope."

"That's about what you were," Andy replied, "only it was the worst kind of rope I ever saw. Those snake-trees are terrible things. I've read of 'em, but I never saw one before. The book that told of them says they squeeze their victims to death just as a snake does. The only way to do is to make some smoke and fire at the bottom. This sort of kills the branches or makes them stupid and they let go. The trees are half animal, and awful things. I hope we don't meet with any more."

"Same here," added Jack fervently, as he grasped Andy's hand, and thanked him for saving his life.

"Do you think you can go on, or shall we return to the ship?" the professor asked.

"Oh I can trail along, if you move a little slowly," Jack replied. "I'm a bit stiff, that's all."

So they resumed their journey. They had gone, perhaps, three miles when Washington, who was in the lead, suddenly stopped and called:

"Sounds like thunder."

The others listened. Sure enough there was a dull rumble and roar audible. It seemed off to the left, but they could see no clouds in the sky, nor any signs of a storm.

"Let's take a walk over that way and see what it is," Mr. Henderson suggested.

As they walked on the noise became louder, until in about half an hour it was like the sound from a blast furnace.

"What do you suppose it can be?" asked Mark.

"Perhaps some new freak of nature," the professor replied. "We seem to have a good many of them here."

They were all on their guard now, for there was no telling into what danger they might run. As they went up a little hill the noise became much louder. The professor and Andy, who had taken the lead, kept a sharp lookout ahead, that they might not unexpectedly fall into some hidden stream or lake. As they topped the hill they saw before them a deep valley, and in the midst of it was that which was causing the roaring sound.

From the centre of an immense mound of rock and earth there spouted up a great column of water, three hundred feet or more, as straight as a flag staff. It was about ten feet in diameter, and at the top it broke into a rosette of sparkling liquid, which as the vari-colored lights played on it, resembled some wonderful flower.

"It's a great geyser!" the professor exclaimed. "We have come to a place like Yellowstone Park. We must be very careful. The crust may be very thin here, and let us down into some boiling spring."

The others gathered around the professor, and, from a safe distance watched the ever rising and falling shaft of water.

It was not regular in motion. Sometimes it would shoot up to a great distance, nearly a thousand feet, the professor estimated. Again it would sink down, as the power sending it out lessened, until it was only a few hundred feet above the rounded top of the mound from which it spurted. But it never fell below this. All the while there was the constant roaring sound, as though the forces of nature below the surface were calling to be let out.

"I hope there are not many of those about," Mr. Henderson remarked after a pause. "If the ship should hit one during the night it would be all up with us. We must keep a careful look-out."

The spouting column had a fascination which held them to the spot for some time. From the hill they had a good view of the surrounding country, but did not see any more geysers.

"Do you think it is hot water?" asked Mark.

"There is no vapor," the professor answered, "but most of the geysers are produced by the action of steam in the interior of the earth. However we'll not take any chances by investigating. I fear it would not be safe to go into that valley."

"Look there!" cried Andy. "I guess we're better off here!" He pointed a little to the right of where the water spouted. The others looked, and saw, coming from a hole in the ground, some shaggy black object.

"What is it?" asked Jack.

"It looks like a bear," replied the hunter, "but I never saw one like it before."

Nor had any of the others, for the creature was a terrible one. It had the body of a bear, but the feet and legs were those of an alligator, while the tail trailed out behind like a snake, and the head had a long snout, not unlike the trunk of an elephant. The creature was about ten feet long and five feet in height.

"Let me try a shot at it!" exclaimed Andy. "That is something worth shooting," and he cocked his rifle.

"Don't!" exclaimed the professor shortly. "You might only wound it, and it would pursue us. We are not ready to fight such creatures as that, and you are the only one armed."

"I never missed anything I aimed at yet," said Andy, a little hurt that any one should doubt his ability to kill at the first shot.

"Perhaps not, but how do you know but what this creature has a bullet proof armor under its hide. This is a strange world, Andy. It is better to take no chances."

"I hate to see him get away," the hunter said.

But, as it happened, the beast was not to get away. As they watched they saw the horrible animal approach the mound from which the water spurted. Up the sides it climbed.

"I guess he's going to get a drink," said Mark.

That was evidently the beast's intention. It went close to the spouting column of water, and thrust its head out so that its tongue could lap from the side. It seemed to have been in the habit of doing this.

For once, and for the last time, however, it made a mistake. The water seemed to veer to one side. In its eagerness to get a drink the animal took another step forward. At that moment the direction of the column changed again, and it tilted over toward the beast.

Suddenly, as the travelers watched, the full force of the big column caught the beast just under the fore shoulders. Up into the air the creature shot, propelled by thousands of pounds pressure. Right up to the top of the column it went, and this time the water rose a thousand feet into the air.

Up and up went the animal, struggling to get away from the remorseless grip. Then, when the water had reached its height, it shot the beast off to one side. Then the brute began to fall, twisting, turning, wiggling and struggling. Down it came with a thud that could be heard above the noise of the geyser.

"I reckon that finishes him," observed Andy. And it had, for there was not a sign of life from the creature.

"I guess we have seen enough for one morning," the professor said, "Let's go back to the airship. It must be nearly dinner time."

They started away. Mark gave a last look at the queer column of water and the dead body of the strange animal. As he passed down the hill he thought he saw the creature move, and stayed to see if this was so. But a second glance convinced him he was mistaken.

The others had gone on and were some distance ahead. Mark hurried on to join them. As he got a last glance at the top of the column, over the brow of the hill, he happened to look off to the left. There was another hill, about the size of the one they had been on.

And, as Mark looked he saw something move. At first he thought it was another beast. But, to his terror he saw that the creature had only two legs, and that it stood upright like a man, but such a man as Mark had never seen before, for he was nearly twelve feet tall.

He was about to cry out and warn the others, when the thing, whatever it was, sunk down, apparently behind some tall bushes, and disappeared as if the earth had opened and swallowed it.

"I wonder if I had better tell them," thought Mark. "I can't show them anything. I wonder if I really saw it, or if it was only a shadow. I guess I'll say nothing. But it is very strange."

Then he hurried on to join the others.

"What makes you so pale?" asked Jack of his chum.

"Nothing," said Mark, somewhat confused. "I guess I'm a little tired, that's all."

They reached the ship in safety, and, having dinner started the machinery and took the Mermaid up into the air.

"We'll travel on and see if we can't find some human beings," the professor said.

All that afternoon they sailed, the country below them unfolding like a panorama. They passed over big lakes, sailing on the surface of some, and over rivers, and vast stretches of forest and dreary plains. But they never saw a sign of human inhabitants.

It was getting on to five o'clock, the hour when the brilliant lights usually disappeared, when Mark, who was steering in the conning tower, gave a cry.

"What is it?" asked the professor, looking up from a rude map he was making of the land they had just traversed.

"It looks like a town before us," said the boy.

Mr. Henderson and Jack looked to where Mark pointed. A few miles ahead and below them were great mounds, not unlike that from which the geyser had spouted. But they were arranged in regular form, like houses on a street, row after row of them. And, as they approached nearer, they could see that the mounds had doors and windows to them. Some of the mounds wer rger than others, and some were of double and triple formation.

"It's a city! The first city of the new world!" cried Jack.

"It is a deserted village!" said the professor. "We have found where the people live, but we have not found them." And he was right, for there was not a sign of life about the place, over which the airship was now suspended.

CHAPTER XXIV
THE GIANTS

"L ET'S go down and investigate," suggested Jack.

"Better wait," counseled the professor. "It will soon be dark, and, though we will have moonlight, we can not see to advantage. I think it will be best to keep the ship in the air to-night, and descend in the morning. Then we can look about and decide on what to do."

They all agreed this was the best plan, and, after making a circle above the deserted village, and noting no signs of life, the Mermaid was brought to a halt over the centre of the town, and about three hundred feet above it. There the travelers would be comparatively safe.

It was deemed best to keep watch that night, and so, Mark, Jack, Bill and Tom took turns, though there was nothing for them to do, as not a thing happened. With the first appearance of dawn Mr. Henderson gave orders to have the ship lowered, and it came to rest in the middle of what corresponded to a street in the queer mound village.

"Now to see what kind of people have lived here!" cried Jack. "They must have been a queer lot. Something like the Esquimaux, only they probably had more trouble keeping cool than the chaps up at the north pole do."

Now that they were down among the mound houses, they saw that the dwellings were much larger than they had supposed. They towered high above the boys' heads, and some of them were large enough in area to have accomodated a company of soldiers.

"Say, the chaps who lived in these must have been some pumpkins," said Jack. "Why the ceilings are about fifteen feet high, and the doors almost the same! Talk about giants! I guess we've struck where they used to hang out, at any rate."

The houses were a curious mixture of clay and soft stone. There were doors, with big skins from animals as curtains, and the windows were devoid of glass. Instead of stairs there were rude ladders, and the furniture in the mound houses was of the roughest kind.

There were fire-places in some of the houses, and the blackened and smoked walls showed that they must have been used. In one or two of the houses clay dishes, most of them broken, were scattered about, and the size of them, in keeping with everything else, indicated that those who used them were of no small stature.

"Some of the bowls would do for bath tubs," said Jack, as he came across one or two large ones.

By this time the professor, Bill and Tom had joined the boys, and the five went on with the exploring tour, while Washington and Andy remained in the ship to get breakfast.

"The inhabitants are evidently of a half-civilized race," the professor said. "Their houses, and the manner in which they live, show them to be allied to the Aztecs, though of course they are much larger than that race."

"What's bothering me," Bill said, "is not so much what race they belong to, as what chance we'd stand in a race with them if they took it into their heads to chase after us. I've read that them there Azhandled races----"

"You mean the Aztecs," interrupted the professor.

"Well the Aztecs, then. But I've read they used to place their enemies on a stone altar and cut their hearts out. Now I'm not hankerin' after anything like that."

"Don't be foolish," spoke Mr. Henderson. "Wait until you meet some of the giants, if that is what they are, and then you can decide what to do."

"It may be too late then," remarked Bill in a low tone, and the boys were somewhat inclined to agree with him.

However, there seemed to be no immediate danger, as there was no sign of any of the big people about the village. The adventurers walked about for some time, but made no discoveries that would throw any light on the reason for the place being left uninhabited. It seemed as if there had been a sudden departure from the place, for in a number of the houses the remains of half-cooked meals were seen.

"Well, I think we have noted enough for the time being," the professor remarked, after they had traversed almost half the length of what seemed to be the principal street. "Let's go back to the ship and have something to eat. Washington may have become alarmed at our absence."

They made a circle in order to take in another part of the town on their way back. While passing through a sort of alley, though it was only narrow by comparison with the other thoroughfares that were very wide, Mark came to a place where there was a circular slab of stone, resting on the ground. In the centre was a big iron ring.

"Hello! Here's something new!" he exclaimed. "Maybe it leads to a secret passage, or covers some hidden treasure."

"I guess it will have to continue to cover it then," Jack spoke. "That probably weighs several tons. None of us could move it."

They made their way back to the ship, where they found Washington and Andy discussing the advisability of going off in search of them.

"Breakfast is mighty near spoiled," said the colored man with an injured air.

But the travelers did full justice to the meal, notwithstanding this. Deciding there was nothing to be gained by staying in that vicinity, the professor started the ship off again.

They traveled several hundred miles in the air, and, as the afternoon was coming to a close, Jack, who was in charge of the conning tower, spied, just ahead of them, another village.

"We will descend there for the night," the professor said. "Does there seem to be any sign of life about?"

"None," replied Mark, who was observing through a telescope the town they were approaching. "It's as dead as the other one."

The airship settled down in a field back of some of the mound houses.

"Now for supper!" cried Jack. "I'm as hungry as----"

He stopped short, for, seeming to rise from the very ground, all about the ship, there appeared a throng of men. And such men as they were! For not one was less than ten feet tall, and some were nearly fifteen!

"The giants have us!" cried Bill, as he saw the horde of creatures surrounding the ship.

CHAPTER XXV
HELD BY THE ENEMY

KEEP the doors closed!" cried the professor. "It is our only hope! I will send the ship up again!"

But it was too late. Washington, who had obeyed the signal from the conning tower to shut off the engines, had disconnected most of them so they could not be started again save from the main room. At the same time there came a yell of dismay from the colored man, who had slid back the steel covering of the main side entrance to the Mermaid.

"I'm caught!" cried Washington.

As the professor and the boys hurried from the tower, they could hear a struggle from where Washington was, and his voice calling:

"Let me go! Let me go!"

Reaching the engine room, which opened directly on the side entrance, the professor saw a pair of enormous hands and arms dragging poor Washington, feet first, out of the ship. Bill and Tom were crouched in one corner, pale with fright.

"Wait until I get my gun!" cried Andy, as he ran for his rifle.

"Hold on!" called the professor in a loud voice. "It will be folly to shoot them! We must try strategy!"

Washington's cries ceased as he was drawn entirely from the ship, the giant hands disappearing at the same time.

"Follow me!" yelled Mr. Henderson, running out of the door.

Hardly knowing what they did, the boys went after him, and their hearts almost stopped beating in fright as they saw the terrible things, which, in the glare of the changing lights, were on every side of them.

For the men were very repulsive looking. They there attired in clothes, very similar in cut to those worn by the travelers, and which seemed to be made of some sort of cloth. But they were loose and baggy and only added to the queer appearance of the giants. Veritable giants they were too. Their faces seemed as large as kegs, and they were so clumsy in shape that Mark, even, frightened as he was, exclaimed:

"They look like men made of putty!" At the same time he saw they bore a resemblance to the creature he had observed on the hill top.

"What shall we do?" asked Andy of the professor. "They are really carrying Washington away!"

Three of the giants were dragging the colored man along the ground, while the other terrible beings stood about as if waiting to see the outcome of the first sally.

"I will try to speak to them," Mr. Henderson said. "I know several languages. They may understand one."

But before he could start on his parley a surprising thing happened. There was a struggle in the little group about Washington. The colored man seemed to be fighting, though the odds, it would appear, were too great to enable him to accomplish anything. But, making a desperate effort to escape, Washington quickly wrenched himself free from the giants' hands and then, striking out with his fists, knocked the three down, one after another.

"I never knew Washington was so strong!" exclaimed Jack.

"Nor I," put in Mark. "Why I should think the men could carry him in one arm as if he was a baby."

The three giants rose slowly to their feet. They uttered strange cries, and motioned with their hands toward the professor, the boys, and the others in the crowd.

"Look out! They're goin' t' grab yo'!" cried Washington.

Three of the giants approached Mark, and a like number closed in on Jack.

"Back to the ship!" cried the professor. "We must defend ourselves!"

But by this time the big men had grabbed the two boys. Then a strange thing took place. Mark and Jack, though they felt that the giants must overcome them in a test of strength, struggled with all their might against being captured. They fought, as a cornered rat will fight, though it knows the odds to be overwhelming. But in this case the unexpected happened.

Both boys found they could easily break the holds of the giants, and Mark, by a vigorous effort, pushed the three men away from him, one at a time violently so that they fell in a heap, one on top of the other.

"Hurrah! We can fight 'em!" cried Mark. "Don't be afraid. They're like mush! They're putty men!"

And, so it seemed, the giants were. Though big in size they were flabby and had nothing like the muscle they should have had in proportion to their build. They went down like meal sacks and were slow to rise.

Jack, seeing how successful his comrade was, attacked the three giants who were striving to make him a captive. He succeeded in disposing of them, knocking one down so hard that the man was unable to rise until his companions helped him.

"That's the way!" cried Washington. "They're soft as snow men!"

The vanquished giants set up a sort of roar, which was answered by their fellows, and soon there was a terrible din.

"All get together!" called the professor. "They are evidently going to make a rush for us. If we stand by one another we may fight them off, though they outnumber us a hundred to one. Besides it will soon be dark, and we may be able to escape!"

Washington, Jack and Mark retreated toward the ship, in the direction of which the others had also made their way. The big men had gathered in a compact mass and were advancing on the adventurers.

"What do you suppose makes them so soft?" asked Mark. "I believe I could manage half a dozen."

"It must be the effect of the climate and conditions here," the professor replied. "Probably they have to be big to stand the pressure of the thick water, and the increased attraction of gravitation. Then too, being without the weight of the atmosphere to which we are accustomed, they have probably expanded. If they were to go up to earth, they might shrink to our size."

"Do you think that possible?"

"Of course. Why do you ask?"

"Nothing in particular," replied Mark. But to himself, he added: "That would explain it all."

It was getting dusk now. The travelers had reached their ship, and rushed inside and tried to close the doors in the face of the advancing horde. But, by this time the giants were so close that one or two of them thrust their big feet in, and prevented this movement. At the same time they set up a great howling.

"Quick!" cried the professor. "We must start the ship and get away!"

"I can't close the door!" yelled Washington, who had been the last to enter.

"Never mind that! Go up with it open! Drag them along if they won't let go!" answered Mr. Henderson, as he ran toward the engine room.

There was a sudden rush among the giants, and a sound as if something was being thrown over the top and ends of the ship. Mark turned the gas machine on, while Jack worked the negative gravity apparatus. They waited for the ship to rise.

"Why don't we go up?" asked the professor.

"'Cause they've caught us!" called out Washington.

"Caught us? How?"

"They've thrown ropes over the top and ends of the ship, and fastened them to their big houses!"

Running to a side window the professor saw that the Mermaid was fastened down by a score of cables, each one six inches thick. They were held captives by the enemy.

CHAPTER XXVI
A FRIEND INDEED

THOUGH the giants, man for man, were no match for the travelers, collectively the horde proved too much. They had swarmed about the ship, and, by passing the big cables over her, effectively held her down.

"Let me get out and I'll cut 'em!" cried Andy. "We must get away from these savages!"

"No, no, don't go out!" exclaimed the professor. "They would eventually kill you, though you might fight them off for a time. We must wait and see what develops. They can have no object in harming us, as we have not injured them."

"I'd rather fight 'em," insisted the old hunter.

But the professor had his way and Andy was forced to obey. The giants had withdrawn their big feet from the side door and Washington had closed it. But nothing else had been accomplished, and the ship could not rise. The gas and negative gravity machines were stopped, as they were only under a useless strain.

Suddenly, the colored lights which had been growing dimmer and dimmer, with the approach of night, went out altogether. Almost as suddenly, Mark, who was watching the giants from the conning tower, as they made fast the loose ends of the cables, saw them make a dash for the mound houses.

"They're afraid of the dark!" he cried. "Come on! We can go out now and loosen the ropes!"

He hurried to tell the professor what he had noticed.

"Good!" exclaimed Mr. Henderson. "Perhaps we can escape now!"

They waited a few minutes, listening to the sound of many big feet running away from the ship, and then, Bill cautiously opened the side door. The others were behind him, waiting, with knives and hatchets in their hands, to rush out and cut the restraining cables.

"All ready!" called Bill. "There doesn't seem to be a one in sight!"

He stepped out but no sooner had he set foot on the ground than there came a thud, and Bill went down as if some one had knocked his feet from under him.

"Go back! Go back!" he cried. "They hit me with something. I'm being smothered!"

"Bring a light!" cried the professor, for the sally had been started in the dark.

Jack brought the portable electric it having been repaired and flashed it out of the door. In the gleam of it, Bill was seen lying prostrate, half covered by an orange, about half as big as himself. The fruit was as soft and mushy as some of the giants themselves, or Bill would not have fared so easily.

Then, as the others stood watching, and while Bill arose and wiped some of the juice from his face, there came a regular shower of the monstrous oranges.

"Get inside quick! We'll be smothered under them!" Mr. Henderson cried.

Pausing only to rescue Bill, the adventurers retreated inside the ship, and made fast the door. Outside they could hear the thud as the oranges were thrown, some hitting the Flying Mermaid and many dropping all about her.

"I guess they are going to have things their own way," observed Bill, as he gazed down on his clothes, which were covered with juice from the fruit.

The night was one of anxiety. The travelers took turns standing guard, but nothing more occurred. The giants remained in their houses, and the heavy ropes still held the ship fast.

"We must hold a council of war," the professor decided as they gathered at breakfast, which was far from a cheerful meal.

With the return of the colored lights the giants again made their appearance. They came swarming from the mound houses, and a great crowd they proved to be. Several thousand at least, Jack estimated, and when he went up into the conning tower and took a survey he could see the strange and terrible creatures pouring in from the surrounding country.

"I'm afraid there will be trouble," he said, as he came down and reported what he had seen.

"We must hold a council of war," repeated the professor. "Has any one anything to suggest?"

"Get a lot of powder and blow 'em up!" cried Andy.

"Arrange electric wires and shock 'em to death!" was Bill's plan.

"Can't we slip the ropes in some way and escape?" asked Jack. "I don't believe we can successfully fight the giants. They are too many, even if they are weak, individually."

"I think you're right there," Mr. Henderson said. "We must try some sort of strategy, but what? That is the question."

For a few minutes no one spoke. They were all thinking deeply, for their lives might hang in the balance.

"I think I have a plan," said Mark, at length. "Did we bring any diving suits with us?"

"There may be one or two," the professor replied. "But what good will they do?"

"Two of us could put them on," continued Mark, "and, as they afford good protection from any missiles like fruit, we could crawl out on the deck of the ship. From there, armed with hatchets or knives we could cut the ropes. Then the ship could rise."

"That's a good plan!" cried the scientist. "We'll try it at once."

Search revealed that two diving suits were among the stores of the Mermaid. Jack and Mark wanted to be the ones to don them, but as the suits were rather large, and as the professor thought it would take more strength than the boys had to do the work, it was decided that Andy and Washington should make the attempt to cut the ropes.

The hunter and colored man lost little time in getting into the modern armor. In the meanwhile Jack, who had been posted as a lookout, reported that there seemed to be some activity among the giants. They were running here and there, and some seemed to be going off toward the woods, that were not far away.

"Now work quickly," urged the professor. "We will be on the watch, and as soon as the last rope is cut we will start the machinery and send the ship up. We will not wait for you to come back inside, so hold fast as best you can when the Mermaid rises."

"We will," answered Andy, just before the big copper helmet was fastened on his head, and Washington nodded to show he understood.

The two who were to attempt the rescue of their comrades were soon on deck. In the conning tower Jack and the professor kept anxious watch, while Mark, Bill and Tom were at the various machines, ready, at the signal, to start the engines.

The giants had now become so interested in whatever plan they had afoot, that they paid little attention to the ship. Consequently Washington and Andy, crawling along the deck in their diving suits, did not, at first attract any attention.

In fact they had cut several of the big ropes, and it began to look as if the plan would succeed, particularly as they were partly hidden from view by the upper gas holder. They were working with feverish haste, sawing away at the big cables with keen knives.

"I guess we'll beat 'em yet!" cried Jack.

"I hope so," replied the professor. "It looks----"

He stopped short, for at that moment a cry arose from the midst of the giants, and one of them pointed toward the ship. An instant later the air was darkened with a flight of big oranges, which the queer creatures seemed to favor as missiles. Probably they found stones too heavy.

"Well, those things can't hurt 'em much with those heavy suits on," observed Mr. Henderson. "There, Washington got one right on the head that time, and it didn't bother him a bit."

Jack had seen the fruit strike the big copper helmet and observed that the colored man only moved his head slightly in order to get rid of the orange.

In fact the giants, seeing for themselves that this mode of warfare was not going to answer, since the two men on the ship continued to cut the restraining cables, gave it up. There was a good deal of shouting among them, and a number ran here and there, seemingly gathering up long poles.

"I wonder if they are going to try the flailing method, and beat poor Andy and Washington," said Mr. Henderson. "It looks so."

The two rescuers were now about a quarter through their hard task. The throwing of the oranges had ceased. But the giants were up to a new trick. They divided into two sections, one taking up a position on one side of the ship, and the other on the opposite. There were about two hundred in each crowd, while the others in the horde drew some distance back.

"They're up to some queer dodge," observed Jack. "What are they placing those sticks to their mouths for?"

The professor observed the throng curiously for a few seconds. Then he exclaimed:

"They are using blow-guns! They are going to shoot arrows at Washington and Andy! We must get them in at once!"

He darted toward a door that opened from the conning tower out on the deck.

"Don't go!" cried Jack. "It's too late! They are beginning to blow!"

He pointed to the throng of giants. The professor could see their cheeks puffed out as the big creatures filled their lungs with air and prepared to expel it through the hollow tubes.

Then there came a sound as if a great wind was blowing. It howled and roared over the ship, not unlike a hurricane in its fury. But there was no flight of arrows through the air, such as would have come from regular blow guns.

"That is strange," said the professor. He thought for a moment. "I have it!" he cried. "They are trying to blow Washington and Andy, off the ship by the power of their breaths! They are not blowing arrows at them! My, but they must have strong lungs!"

And, in truth, that was the plan of the giants. The hollow tubes, made from some sort of big weed, sent a blast of air at the two men on the ship's deck, that made them lie flat and cling with both hands to avoid being sent flying into the midst of the giants, on one side or the other. But the giants had reckoned without the weight of the diving suits, and it was those, with the big lead soles of the shoes, that helped to hold Washington and Andy in place.

"Come back! Came back!" cried the professor, opening the conning tower door and calling to the two brave men. "Come back, both of you! Do you hear?"

As the portal slid back the rush of air was almost like that of a cyclone. Then it suddenly ceased, as the giants saw their plan was not likely to succeed.

But now there arose from the outer circle of the horde a shout of triumph. It was caused by the return of those who had, a little while before, hurried off to the woods. They came back bearing big trees, tall and slender, stripped of their branches, so that they resembled flag staffs. It took a dozen giants to carry each one.

The whole throng was soon busy laying the poles in a row in front of the ship.

"What can they be up to now?" asked Jack.

"It looks as if they were going to slide the ship along on rollers," the professor replied.

Sure enough this was the giant's plan. A few minutes later those in the Mermaid felt her moving forward, as the giants, massed behind, shoved. On to the poles she slid. The ropes were loosened to permit this, but not enough to enable the boat to rise.

Then the travelers felt the ship being lifted up.

"They are going to carry us away, with the poles for a big stretcher!" cried the professor.

Looking from the side windows the boys saw that a great crowd of the big men were on either side of the Mermaid, each giant grasping a pole, and lifting. Farther out were others, holding the ends of the cables which Washington and Andy had not succeeded in cutting.

The ship was being carried along by a thousand or more giants, as the ancient warriors, slain in battle, were carried home on the spears of their comrades.

"This is the end of the Mermaid!" murmured Mr. Henderson in sorrowful tones.

As they looked from the conning tower the professor and the two boys observed a commotion among the leaders of the giants. They seemed to be wavering. Suddenly the forward part of the ship sank, as those ahead laid their poles down on the ground. Then those behind did the same, and the Mermaid, came to a stop, and once more rested on the earth.

"What does this mean?" asked the scientist in wonder.

All at once the entire crowd of giants threw themselves down on their faces, and there, standing at the bow of the ship, was a giant, half again as large as any of the others. He was clad in a complete suit of golden armor on which the changing lights played with beautiful effect, and in his hand he held an immense golden sword. He pointed the weapon at the ship as if he had raised it in protection, and his hand was stretched in commanding gesture over the prostrate giants.

"Perhaps he has come to save us!" cried Mark.

CHAPTER XXVII
A GREAT JOURNEY

SUCH indeed, seemed to be the case. The golden-armored giant, after standing for a few moments in an attitude of command, waved his sword three times about his head, and uttered a command, in a voice that sounded like thunder. Then the prostrate ones arose, and, making low bows hurried away in all directions.

Watching them disappear, the golden one sheathed his weapon and approached the ship. He caught sight of the professor and the two boys in the conning tower, for Mark had gone there when he found the ship being transported, and held up his two hands, the palms outward.

"It is the sign of peace in the language all natives employ," said the professor. "I think I shall trust him."

Followed by the boys he descended from the little platform in the tower, and to the door that opened on the deck.

"Shall we go out?" he asked.

"We can't be much worse off," replied Mark. "Let's chance it."

So, not without many misgivings, they slid back the portal and stepped out to face the strange and terrible being who had so suddenly come to their rescue.

The giant in the golden armor did not seem surprised to see them. In fact he acted as though he rather expected them. He continued to hold up one hand, with the palm, outward, while, with the other, he removed his helmet and bowed low. Then he cast his sword on the ground and advanced toward the ship. When within ten feet he sat down on the ground, and this brought his head nearer the earth, so that his auditors could both see and hear him to better advantage.

As soon as the giant saw the travelers were outside their ship he began to speak to them in a voice, which, though he might have meant it to be low and gentle, was like the bellowing of a bull. At the same time he made many gestures, pointing to the ship, to himself and to Mark.

"What is he saying, professor?" asked Jack.

"I can't understand all he says," Mr. Henderson replied. "He uses some words derived from the Latin and some from the Greek. But by piecing it out here and there, and by interpreting his motions I am able to get at something."

"And what is it all about?"

"It is a strange story," the scientist replied. "He has only gone about half way through it. Wait until he finishes and I will tell you."

The golden-armored giant, who had stopped in his narrative while Jack was speaking, resumed. His gestures became more rapid, and his words came faster. Several times Mr. Henderson held up his hand for him to cease, while he puzzled out what was meant.

At one point, the professor seemed much startled, and motioned for the strange being to repeat the last part of his discourse. When this had been done Mr. Henderson shook his head as though in doubt.

At length the story was finished, and the lone giant, for there were no others in sight now, folded his arms and seemed to await what the professor's answer might be. Mr. Henderson turned to the boys, and to the others of the Mermaid's company, who, by this time, had joined him, and said:

"Friends, I have just listened to a strange story. It is so strange that, but for the fact that our own adventures are verging on the marvelous, I could hardly believe it. In the first place, this man here is the king of this country. That is why all the other natives obeyed him.

"In the second place it seems he has been a passenger in our boat, and came here from the earth's surface with us!"

"What's that?" cried Jack.

"That explains the strange happenings!" ejaculated Mark. "No wonder I could never solve the secret of the storeroom."

"You are right, it does," replied Mr. Henderson. "I will not go into all the details of how it happened, but it seems the big hole through which we came is only one of two entrances to this inner world. Rather it is the entrance, and there is another, close to it, which is the exit. Through the latter a big stream of water spouts up, just as one pours down through the opening we used.

"Hankos, which is the name of the king, was for many years a student of science. He longed to see where the big stream of upward spurting water went, and wanted to know whence came the down-pouring one. So he undertook a daring experiment.

"He constructed a great cylinder, and, keeping his plans a secret, conveyed it to the spouting water, entered it, and, by means of pulleys and levers, after he had shut himself inside, cast himself into the up-shooting column. He took along compressed air cylinders to supply an atmosphere he could breathe, and some food to eat, for it appears our giant friends are something of inventors in their way. The current of water bore him to the surface of the earth, and he was cast up on the ocean, in what was probably taken for a waterspout if any one saw it.

"Then a strange thing happened. No sooner did Hankos open his cylinder, which served him as a boat, than he lost his gigantic size, owing to the difference of the two atmospheres. He became almost of the same size as ourselves, except that his skin hung in great folds on him, and he seemed like a wrinkled old man. His clothes too, were a world too large.

"He had a terrible time before he reached shore, and a hard one after it, for his strange appearance turned almost every one against him. He was sorry he had ventured to solve the mystery of the up-shooting stream of water, for he was worse than an outcast.

"Then he began to plan to get back to his own inner world. But he could not find the downward stream, and, not knowing the language of the countries where he landed, he had no means of ascertaining. He traveled from place to place, always seeking for something that would lead him back to his own country.

"Finally he heard of us, and of our ship, though how I do not know, as I thought I had kept it a great secret. By almost superhuman struggles he made his way to our island. He says he concealed himself aboard the Mermaid the night before we sailed, but I hardly believe it possible. It seems----"

"He did it, for I saw him!" interrupted Mark.

"You saw him!" cried Mr. Henderson.

Then Mark told of the many things that had puzzled him so, how he had seen the queer figure slinking aboard the boat, of the disappearance of food from time to time, and of the strange noises in the storeroom.

"That bears out what he told me," the professor said. "Hankos says he used to steal out nights and take what food he could get, and he also mentions some one, answering to Mark's description, who nearly discovered him once as he hurried back into the apartment.

"However, it seems to be true, since Mark confirms it. At any rate Hankos stayed in hiding, and made the entire trip with us, and, just as we all became overcome with the strange gas he escaped, having begun to expand to his original giant size, and being unable to remain any longer in his cramped quarters."

"That's so, he did!" cried Mark. "I saw him come out of the place just before I lost my senses. It was a terrible sight, and none of you would believe me when I told you some of the occurrences afterward."

"You must forgive us for that," the professor said. "We have learned much since then."

"What did Hankos do after he left the ship when it landed in this country?" asked Jack.

"He traveled until he came to this village, which is the chief one of this country," replied the professor. "Part of the time he followed us at a distance, being able to travel very fast."

Mark remembered the strange figure of a giant he had seen on the hill tops several times, and knew that he had been observing the being who had played such a queer part in their lives.

"When he came back among his own people," went on Mr. Henderson, "they would not receive him at first, believing him to be an impostor. But Hankos convinced them of his identity and was allowed to don the golden armor, which is the badge of kingship. He had only been in office for a little while when he heard of the arrival of the strange thing, which turned out to be our ship. He recognized it from the description, and, learning that we were likely to be sacrificed to the fury and ignorance of the giants, he hurried here and saved our lives.

"He says he can never thank us enough for being the means whereby he was able to get back to his own country, and says the freedom of this whole inner world is ours. He has given orders that we are to go wherever we like, and none will molest us. He tells me the land is a wonderful one, compared to our own, and urges us to make a long journey. He would like to go with us, only, now that he has resumed his natural size, he can not get inside the ship."

"Hurrah for King Hankos!" cried Jack and the others joined him in a hearty cheer.

The giant in the golden armor evidently understood the compliment which was paid him, for he waved his helmet in the air and responded with a shout of welcome that made the ground tremble.

Hankos waited until the professor had translated all of the story to the other travelers. Then the genial giant began to talk some more, and the professor listened intently.

"He says," spoke Mr. Henderson to his friends, "that we will be supplied with all the fruit we want, and with the best of the houses to sleep in on our journey. He also tells me he has great stores of shining stones and piles of the metal of which his armor is made, and that we are welcome to as much as we want. If this means unlimited gold and diamonds, we may make our fortunes."

"Jest let me git ma' hand on a few sparklers an' I'll quit work!" exclaimed Washington.

"I have told him," the scientist went on, "that we will take advantage of his kind offer. We will start on our trip in a day or so, after we have looked over the ship to see if it is not damaged. He tells me the gold and sparkling stones are several thousand miles away, on top of a high mountain. We will make that our objective point."

The interview between the king and Mr. Henderson having ended, the former waved his sword in the air and the swarm of big men came back. They had been hiding back in the woods. Now their manner was very different. They carefully removed the rollers and ropes, and soon there was brought to the adventurers an immense pile of fine fruits. If our friends had stayed there a year they could not have eaten it all. The giants were judging the appetites of the travelers by their own.

That night the adventurers slept more soundly than they had since entering the strange world. They felt they had nothing to fear from the giants. In the morning they were not molested, though big crowds gathered to look at the ship. But they kept back a good distance. The machinery was found to be in good shape, save for a few repairs, and when these were made, the professor announced he would start on a long journey.

For several weeks after that the travelers swung about in their ship, sometimes sailing in the air and again on big seas and lakes viewing the wonders of the inner world. They were many and varied, and the professor collected enough material for a score of books which he said he would write when he got back to the outer world once more.

One afternoon, as they were sailing over a vast stretch of woodland, which did not seem to be inhabited, Mr. Henderson, looking at one of the gages on the wall, asked:

"Boys do you know how far you have traveled underground?"

"How far?" asked Jack, who hated to guess riddles.

"More than four thousand miles," was the answer.

"But we haven't come to that mountain of gold and diamonds," said Mark. "I am anxious to see that."

"Have patience," replied the professor. "I have not steered toward it yet. There are other things to see."

Just then Washington's voice could be heard calling from the conning tower:

"We're coming to a big mountain!"

CHAPTER XXVIII
THE TEMPLE OF TREASURE

WHAT'S that?" fairly yelled the professor.

"We am propelling ourselves in a contiguous direction an' in close proximity to an elevated portion of th' earth's surface which rises in antiguous proximity t' th' forward part of our present means of locomotion!" said the colored man in a loud voice.

"Which means there may be a collision," the professor said, as he and the boys hurried toward the tower,

"Jest what I said," retorted Washington. "What'll I do?"

"Send the ship a little higher," answered Mr. Henderson. "We mustn't hit any mountains."

Washington forced more gas into the holder, and speeded the negative gravity machine up some, so that the Mermaid, which was flying rather low, ascended until it was in no danger of colliding with the peak which reared its lofty height just ahead of them.

As the ship sailed slowly over the mountain, Mark gazed down and exclaimed:

"Doesn't that look like the ruins of some building?"

The professor took a pair of field glasses from a rack in the wall and took a long view.

"It must be the place," he said in a low voice.

"What place?" asked Jack.

"The temple of treasure," was the answer. "Hankos told me it was on top of the highest mountain in the land, and this must be it, for it is the loftiest place we have seen. But we must be careful, for there is danger down there."

"What kind?" asked Mark.

"The place was long ago deserted by the giants," Mr. Henderson went on. "Ages ago it was one of their storehouses for treasure, but there were wars among themselves, Hankos said, and this part of the country was laid waste. Savage beasts took up their abode in the temple, and since then, in spite of the great size of the giants, they have not dared to venture here. If we brave the animals we may have all the gold and diamonds we can take away."

"Then for one, I'm willin' t' go down an' begin th' extermination at once," put in Andy. "I've always wanted t' be rich."

"We must proceed cautiously," the professor said. "We are ill prepared to fight any such beasts as we saw at the big geyser. At the same time they may have deserted this place. I think we will lower the ship down over the temple, and spend several hours in observation. Then, if nothing develops, we can enter and see if the treasure is there."

This plan was voted a good one, and the Mermaid after having been steered directly over the ruined temple, was brought to a halt, and enough gas let out so that it fell to about fifty feet in the air above it.

The adventurers began their watch. The afternoon waned and there were no signs of any beasts in or about the temple.

"I reckon we can take a chance," said Andy, who was anxious to get his hands on some diamonds.

"Better wait until morning," counseled Mr. Henderson. "It will soon be dark, and it doesn't look like a nice place to go stumbling about in by moonlight."

So, though all but the scientist were anxious, they had to wait until the night had passed. Several times Washington got up to see if the temple had, by any chance, taken wings during the long hours of darkness, but each time he found it was still in place.

"Seems laik it'll never come mornin'." he said.

But dawn came at length, and, after a hasty breakfast, preparations to enter the temple were made. Andy loaded his gun for "bear" as he expressed it, and the boys each took a revolver.

The ship was lowered to as level a place as could be found, and then, seeing that everything was in readiness for a quick departure, the professor led the way out of the Mermaid.

The entrance to the temple was through a big arched gateway. Some of the stones had fallen down, and the whole structure looked as if it might topple over at any moment.

"Go carefully," cautioned Mr. Henderson, "Watch on all sides and up above. Better let Andy and me go ahead."

The scientist and the old hunter led the way. Through the arch they went, and emerged into what must at one time have been a magnificent courtyard. Before them was the temple proper, a vast structure, with an opening through which fifty men might have marched abreast. But the doors were gone, and the portal was but a black hole.

"I hope there ain't any ghosts in there," said Washington, with a shiver.

"Nonsense!" exclaimed the professor. "There may be things as bad, but there are no such things as ghosts. Have your gun ready, Andy."

With every sense on the alert, the old hunter advanced. Every one was a bit nervous, and, as Mark and Jack afterward admitted, they half expected some terrible beast to rush out at them. But nothing of the kind happened, and they went into the interior of the temple.

At first it was so dark they could see nothing. There were vast dim shapes on every side, and from the hollow echo of their footsteps they judged the roof must be very high and the structure big in every way.

Then, as their eyes became used to the darkness, they could make out, up front, something like an altar or pulpit.

"Perhaps that's where they offered up the gold and diamonds as a sacrifice to their gods," spoke Mark in a whisper.

"Sacrifice to their gods!" came back a hundred echoes and the sound made every one shudder.

"Oh!" said Washington, in a low voice.

"Oh! Oh! Oh!" repeated the echoes in voices of thunder.

"Well, this is pleasant," spoke Andy, in his natural tones, and, to the surprise of all there was no echo. It was only when a person whispered or spoke low that the sound was heard. After that they talked naturally.

"You stay here, and Andy and I will go up front and see what there is," said Mr.

Henderson. "Be on your guard, and if you hear us coming back in a hurry, run!"

It was with no little feeling of nervousness that the boys, Bill, Tom and Washington watched the two men move off in the darkness. They could hear their footsteps on the stone flags and could dimly see them.

"They must be almost to the altar by this time," said Mark, after a long pause.

Hardly had he spoken than there came a loud, sound from where Mr. Henderson and Andy had gone. It was as if some giant wings were beating the air. Then came shrill cries and the voice of the old hunter could be heard calling:

"Kneel down, Professor! Let me get a shot at the brute!"

Those waiting in the rear of the temple huddled closer together. What terrible beast could have been aroused?

The next instant the place seemed illuminated as if by a lightning flash, and a sound as of a thousand thunder claps resounded.

"I think I winged him!" cried Andy's voice, and the boys knew he had fired at something.

Then there came a crash, and from the roof of the old temple a dozen stones toppled off to one side, letting in a flood of colored light.

By this illumination could be seen, flapping through the big space overhead, an enormous bat, as large as three eagles. And, as it flew about in a circle it gave utterance to shrill cries.

"Bang!" Andy's gun spoke again, and the bat with a louder cry than before, darted through the hole in the roof made by the falling stones, which had been loosened by the concussion from the rifle.

"Come on!" cried the old hunter. "That was the guardian of the treasure! We are safe now!"

Then, in the light which streamed through the broken roof, the adventurers could see, heaped up on a great altar, behind which sat a horrible graven image, piles of yellow metal, and sparkling stones. In little heaps they were, arranged as if offerings to the terrible god of the giants. There were bars and rings of gold, dishes of odd shape, and even weapons. As for the sparkling stones, they were of many colors, but the white ones were more plentiful than all the others.

"Gold and diamonds! Diamonds and gold!" murmured the professor. "There is the ransom of many kings in this ancient temple."

"Wish I had a big bag!" exclaimed Washington, as he began filling all his pockets with the precious metal and gems. "If I had a-thought I'd have brought a dress-suit case!"

"A dress-suit case full of diamonds!" exclaimed Mark.

Then he too, as did all the others, fell to filling his pockets with the wealth spread so lavishly before them. There was the riches of a whole world in one place and no one but themselves to take it.

For several minutes no one spoke. The only sound was the rattle of the stones and the clink of gold, and when some of the diamonds dropped on the floor they did not bother to gather them up. There were too many on the altar.

"We will be rich for life!" gasped old Andy, who had been poor all his years.

"I can't carry any more!" gasped Washington. "I'm goin' back for----"

What he was going back for he never said, for, at that instant, happening to look up at the hole in the roof, he gave a startled try:

"Here come the terrible bats!"

They all gazed upward. Through the opening they could see a great flock of the awful birds, headed for the temple, and they were led by one which seemed to fly with difficulty. It was the guardian of the treasure that Andy had wounded.

"Quick! We must get out of here!" shouted the old hunter. "They are big enough and strong enough to tear us all to pieces. Hurry!"

Down the centre of the temple they rushed, and not a moment too soon, for, ere they had passed half way to the entrance, the opening in the roof was darkened by the coming of the bats, and soon the flapping of their wings awoke the thundering echoes in the ruined structure, while their shrill cries struck terror to the hearts of the travelers.

Up to the altar circled the bats, and then wheeling they flapped down the dim aisles toward the adventurers.

"Hurry! Hurry!" shouted Andy, who was in the rear.

He raised his rifle and fired several shots into the midst of the terrible creatures.

A number of the bats were wounded, and the others were so frightened by the sound of the shots and the flashes of fire that they turned back. This enabled the fleeing ones to gain the entrance to the temple, and soon they were outside.

"To the ship!" yelled Bill.

"There's little danger now!" called Andy, panting, for the run had winded him. "They will hardly attack us in the light!"

And he was right, for, though they could hear the bats flying about inside the temple, and uttering their cries, none came outside.

But no one felt like staying near the uncanny structure, and little time was lost in reaching the Mermaid. Then the doors were fastened, and the ship was sent high up into the air.

"Which way?" asked Jack, when Mr. Henderson told him to go to the conning tower and steer.

"Back to where we first met the giants," replied the professor. "We must prepare to start for our own earth again soon."

"I've almost forgotten how real sunlight looks," thought Jack, as he headed the ship around the other way. As he turned the levers a big diamond dropped from his pocket and rolled on the floor.

"This will be a good reminder of our trip though," he added.

The travelers, even including Mr. Henderson, were so taken up with their suddenly acquired riches that they hardly thought of meals. At the professor's suggestion they tied their gold and stones up in small packages convenient to carry.

"Better place them where you can grab them in a hurry in case of accident," the old scientist went on. "Of course if there should be too bad an accident they would never be of any use to us down here, but we'll look on the bright side of things."

"Do you anticipate any accident?" asked Jack anxiously.

"No, Oh no," replied Mr. Henderson, but Jack thought the aged man had something weighing on his mind.

CHAPTER XXIX
BACK HOME-- CONCLUSION

O N and on sped the Mermaid. Now that the travelers felt their journey accomplished they were anxious to begin the homeward trip. They made a straight course for the village where they had so nearly met with disaster, and where the king of the giants had saved them. They went in a direct line, and did not travel here and there, as they had after they left the town. Consequently they shortened the route by a great distance. Yet it was long enough, and when they finally came in sight of the place the dial registered a trip of five thousand miles underground.

It was one evening when they landed almost at the spot whence they had taken flight eventually to reach the temple of the treasure. Most of the giants had betaken themselves to their mound houses, but Hankos was walking in the fields, and, when he caught sight of the airship hovering above him he waved his great sword in welcome.

He rushed up to shake hands with the travelers when they came out of the ship, though to greet him it was only possible for the adventurers to grasp one of his immense fingers.

As soon as the greetings were over Hankos began to speak rapidly to the professor, at the same time going through many strange motions.

"It is as I feared!" suddenly exclaimed the scientist.

"What is the matter?" asked Mark.

"The worst has happened!" went on Mr. Henderson. "The great hole by which we came into this place has been closed by an earthquake shock!"

"The hole closed?" repeated Jack.

"An earthquake shock!" murmured Mark.

"Then how are we going to get back to earth?" asked old Andy.

A terrible fear entered the hearts of the travelers. The closing of the opening by which they had come to the strange world meant, in all probability that they would have to spend the rest of their lives in this underground place.

"What good did it do us to get all those diamonds and that gold?" asked Mark in a sorrowful tone.

Hankos began to speak again, using his gestures which were almost as eloquent as words. The professor watched and listened intently. Then there seemed to come a more hopeful look to his face. He nodded vigorously as Hankos went on with what seemed to be an explanation.

"It's worth trying, at all events!" the scientist exclaimed. "It is our only hope!"

"What is?" asked Jack.

"Friends," began the professor in solemn tones. "I must admit our plight is desperate. At the same time there is a bare chance of our getting back to our own earth. As you remember, Hankos went from this place to the upper regions through the upward spouting column of water."

"If we had our submarine we might also," interrupted Jack. "But the Mermaid isn't built to sail in that fashion."

"Nor would the Porpoise have served us in this emergency," said the professor. "It would prove too heavy. But, nevertheless, I think I have a plan. Now, Mark, you are about to learn the secret of the storeroom. The real one, not the hiding of Hankos in there, which you imagined to be the cause of my desire to keep something hidden. When we planned a trip to this underground world I had a dim idea that we might meet with trouble. So I planned and made a cylinder lifeboat."

"A cylinder lifeboat?" repeated Mark.

"Yes," replied Mr. Henderson. "I have it in the storeroom. I did not want any of you to see it for fear you would have faint hearts. I thought there might be no necessity of using it. But, since there is, we must do our best. I will admit it may be a fearful ordeal, but we will have to risk something in order to escape.

"I have in the storeroom a large cylinder, capable of holding us all. It will also contain food and drink for a month, but we will all have to go, packed almost like sardines in a box. My plan is to take the Mermaid to the place where the column of water shoots up. There we will get into the cylinder, close it, and trust ourselves to the terrible force that may bring us back to the upper world. What do you say? Shall we attempt it?"

For a few seconds no one spoke. Then Jack said slowly:

"I don't see that we can do anything else. I don't want to stay here all my life."

"I wants a chance t' wear some of them sparklers," put in Washington.

"Then we will make the attempt," the professor added. "Now all aboard for the place where the water shoots up!"

Questioning Hankos, the professor learned how to reach the strange place. It was in the midst of a desolate country where none of the giants ever went, so afraid were they of the strange phenomenon.

It was a week's journey. Sometimes the Mermaid flew through the air, and again it sailed on vast lakes or inland seas. On the trip they met with big waterfalls and terrible geysers that spouted a mile or more into the air. They traveled by night as well as day, though it was necessary to keep a sharp watch.

Sometimes the ship passed through great flocks of birds that surrounded her and sought to pierce the aluminum hull with their sharp beaks and talons. Over the mountains and valleys the ship sailed until, one evening, there sounded through the air a strange rumbling sound.

"It is thunder," said Old Andy.

"It is the water column," replied the scientist. "We are at the end of our trip. May the remainder be as successful!"

The ship was lowered to the surface, as it was deemed best to approach the column when the lights were shining. No one slept much that night, for the roaring and rumbling never ceased.

In the morning the ship was sent forward slowly. Ever and ever the terrific sound increased, until it was almost deafening. They had to call to each other to be heard.

Then, as the Mermaid passed over a mountain, the adventurers saw, in a valley below them, the up-shooting water.

It was a vast column, nearly three hundred feet in thickness, and as solid and white as a shaft of marble. Up, up, up, it went, until it was lost to sight, but there were no falling drops, and not even a spray came from the watery shafts.

"There is a terrible power to it," the professor said. "May it prove our salvation!"

The ship was lowered about a hundred feet away from the waterspout. All around them the ground was vibrating with the force of the fluid.

"To think that connects with the world above!" exclaimed Jack.

"It's a good thing for us that it does," Mark answered.

"We must lose no time," the professor put in. "If the earthquake destroyed the downward shaft, it may effect this one in time. We must escape while we can."

Then, for the first time, he opened the storeroom and the big cylinder was disclosed to view. It was made of aluminum, and shaped like an immense cigar. The hull was double, and it was strongly braced. Inside were padded berths for the occupants, and there was just room enough for the seven adventurers. Once they had entered they could not move about, but must stay in their little compartment.

Compressed air in strong cylinders furnished a means of breathing, and there were tiny electric lights operated by a storage battery. There was also a chamber to be filled with the lifting gas. The cylinder was so arranged that it would float on it's long axis if thrown into the water. A trap door hermetically sealed gave access to the interior. A small propeller, worked by compressed air, furnished motive power.

The food supply consisted of compressed capsules on which a man could subsist for several days. There was also some water, but not much, since that can not be compressed and would, therefore, take considerable room.

"The only thing for us to do," said the professor, "is to get into the cylinder, seal it up, and trust to Providence. This is what I intended to use when we were caught in the draught."

"How can we get into the column of water after we shut ourselves into the cylinder?" asked Mark.

"The cylinder fits into a sort of improvised cannon," said Mr. Henderson. "It is fired by electricity and compressed air. "We will aim it at the column, press the button and be projected into the midst of the water. Then----" He did not finish the sentence, but the others knew what he meant.

"When are we to start?" asked Mark.

"As soon as possible," replied the professor. "I must arrange the cylinder, compress the air and lay out the food supply."

It took the rest of the day to do this, as the inventor found it would be advisable to attach a weight to the end of the cylinder, to hold it upright in the column of water. The weight could be detached automatically when they were shot up into the midst of the ocean, where, as Hankos had told them, the column spurted forth.

Then some food was stored in the tiny ship that was destined to be their last hope, and some tanks of water were placed in it.

"I think we are almost ready," Mr. Henderson said about noon the next day.

"What about our gold and diamonds?" asked Jack suddenly. "Can we take them with us in the cylinder?"

"That's so!" exclaimed Mr. Henderson. "I forgot about them. I'm afraid we'll have to leave the riches behind. We will not be able to carry them and the food we need, for it may be a week or more before we can leave the cylinder. Gold and diamonds will be a poor substitute for something to eat."

"I'm goin' t' take mine!" said Washington with much conviction. "I might as well starve rich as starve poor!"

"We may be able to take a few diamonds," the professor answered. "The gold will be too heavy. Let each one select the largest of the diamonds he has and put them in his pockets."

Then began a sorting of the wealth. It was strange, as they recalled afterward, throwing away riches that would have made millionaires envious, but it had to be done. All the wealth in the world would not equal a beef capsule when they were starving, and they realized it. So they only saved a few pieces of gold as souvenirs, and took the best of the diamonds. But even then they had a vast fortune with them.

At last all was in readiness. The cylinder had been placed in the tube from which it was to be shot gently forth by compressed air, so that it would fall into the upward spouting column of water. The charge of compressed air was put in and the electric wires arranged.

"Are we all ready?" asked Mr. Henderson.

"I think so," said Jack, in what sounded like a whisper, but which was loud, only the noise of the water muffled it.

"Then we had better enter the cylinder," spoke the inventor. "Take a last look at the Flying Mermaid, boys, for you will never see again the ship that has borne us many thousand miles. She served us well, and might again, but for the freak of nature that has placed us in this position."

For the first time the adventurers realized that they must abandon the craft in which they had reached the new world. So it was with no little feeling of sadness that they climbed up the ladder that had been arranged and slid down into the cylinder. One by one they took their places in the padded berths arranged for them. It was a snug fit, for the professor knew if there was too much room he and the others might be so tossed about as to be killed.

Mr. Henderson was the last to enter. Standing at the manhole he took a final look at his pet creation, the Mermaid. Through the opened windows the colored lights came, shifting here and there. Outside the terrible column of water was roaring as if anxious to devour them.

"Good-bye, Mermaid!" said the professor softly.

Then he closed down the manhole cover and tightened the screws that held it in place. He touched a button that turned on the electric lights and the interior of the cylinder was illuminated with a soft glow.

"Are you all ready?" he asked.

"Jest as much as I ever will be," replied Washington, who, as the crisis approached, seemed more light-hearted than any of the others.

"Then here we go!" exclaimed Mr. Henderson.

His fingers touched the button that connected with the electric machine, which operated the compressed air.

There sounded a muffled report. Then it seemed to those in the cylinder that the end of the world had come. They shot upward and outward, through the top of the conning tower which had been removed. The cylinder, launched straight at the column of water struck it squarely and, an instant later was caught in the grasp of the giant force and hurled toward the upper world.

Up and up and up the mass of metal with its human freight went. Now it was spinning like a top, again it shot toward the earth's crust like an arrow from the archer's bow.

It was moving with the velocity of a meteor, yet because of being surrounded with water, and traveling with the same velocity as the column, there was no friction. Had there been, the heat generated would have melted the case in an instant.

For the first few seconds those in the cylinder were dazed by the sudden rush. Then as it became greater and greater there came a curious dull feeling, and, one after another lost consciousness. The terror of the water column, and the frightful speed, had made them senseless.

It seemed like a month later, though, of course, it could have been only a few hours or a day at most when Jack opened his eyes. He saw his companions, white and senseless all around him, and at first thought they were dead. Then he saw Mark looking at him, and Washington asked:

"Is any one livin' 'sides me?"

"I am," replied Jack decidedly.

Then, one after another they regained their senses. But they were in a strange daze, for they were being carried along like a shooting star, only, as they went at the same rate as did the element carrying them, they did not realize this.

"I think I'm hungry," said Bill, who had the best appetite of any of the travelers.

"You'll find a beef capsule in the little compartment over your head," spoke the professor.

Bill was about to reach for it, when they were all startled by a sudden side motion of the cylinder. Then came a violent shock, and a sound as of splashing water. Next the cylinder seemed to be falling, and, a few minutes later to be shooting upward. Following this there was another splash and the cylinder began to bob about like a cork on a mill pond.

"We have reached the sea! We are afloat on the ocean!" cried the professor.

Hurriedly he disengaged himself from the straps that held him to his bunk. He pushed back the lever that opened the manhole. Into the opening glowed the glorious sunlight, while to the occupants came the breath of salt air.

"Hurrah!" cried Jack. "We are safe at last!"

"Safe at last!" the professor answered, and then they all gave a cheer.

For their cylinder, which might now be termed a boat, was floating on the great Atlantic. The blue sky was overhead and the air of the sea fanned their cheeks.

They had shot up from the underground earth, in the column of water, had been tossed high into the air, had fallen back when the liquid shaft broke into spray, had descended into the ocean, gone down a hundred feet or more, and then had shot up like a cork to bob about the surface.

For a week they were afloat, and then they were picked up by a passing vessel, rather weak and very much cramped, but otherwise in good shape. They said nothing of their adventures, save to explain that they were experimenting in a new kind of boat. About a month later, for the ship that had rescued them was a slow sailer, they were back on the island whence that wonderful voyage was begun.

"Well, we solved the mystery of the center of the earth," remarked Jack, one evening, when they were gathered in the old shack where so many wonderful adventures had been planned.

"Yes, we did," said Mr. Henderson. "And no one else is ever likely to go there."

"Why?"

"Because the only way of getting there was destroyed by the earthquake, and no one could ever force his way down through that upward-shooting column of water."

"That's so. Well, we have the diamonds, anyway," spoke Mark. "They ought to make us rich."

And the jewels did, for the stones proved to be of great value, even though the adventurers had saved only a few of the many they found in the ruined temple.

But there was money enough so that they all could live in comfort; the rest of their lives. As the professor was getting quite old, and incapable of making any more wonderful inventions, he closed up his workshop and settled down to a quiet life. As for Washington, Andy, and Bill and Tom, they invested their money received from the sale of the diamonds in different business ventures, and each one did well.

"I am going in for a good education," said Jack to Mark.

"Just what I am going to do," answered his chum. "And after we've got that----" He paused suggestively.

"We'll go in for inventing airships, or something like that, eh?"

"Yes. We've learned a great deal from Mr. Henderson, and in the course of time we ought to be able to turn out something even more wonderful than the Electric Monarch, the Porpoise, or the Flying Mermaid."

"Yes, and when we've invented something better----"

"We'll take another trip."

"Right you are!"

And then the two chums shook hands warmly; and here we will say good-bye.

The Codes Of Hammurabi And Moses
W. W. Davies

QTY

The discovery of the Hammurabi Code is one of the greatest achievements of archaeology, and is of paramount interest, not only to the student of the Bible, but also to all those interested in ancient history...

Religion   **ISBN:** *1-59462-338-4*   **Pages:132**
MSRP $12.95

The Theory of Moral Sentiments
Adam Smith

QTY

This work from 1749. contains original theories of conscience amd moral judgment and it is the foundation for systemof morals.

Philosophy **ISBN:** *1-59462-777-0*   **Pages:536**
MSRP $19.95

Jessica's First Prayer
Hesba Stretton

QTY

In a screened and secluded corner of one of the many railway-bridges which span the streets of London there could be seen a few years ago, from five o'clock every morning until half past eight, a tidily set-out coffee-stall, consisting of a trestle and board, upon which stood two large tin cans, with a small fire of charcoal burning under each so as to keep the coffee boiling during the early hours of the morning when the work-people were thronging into the city on their way to their daily toil...

Pages:84

Childrens   **ISBN:** *1-59462-373-2*   *MSRP $9.95*

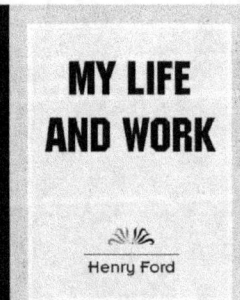

My Life and Work
Henry Ford

QTY

Henry Ford revolutionized the world with his implementation of mass production for the Model T automobile. Gain valuable business insight into his life and work with his own auto-biography... "We have only started on our development of our country we have not as yet, with all our talk of wonderful progress, done more than scratch the surface. The progress has been wonderful enough but..."

Pages:300

Biographies/   **ISBN:** *1-59462-198-5*   *MSRP $21.95*

The Art of Cross-Examination
Francis Wellman

QTY

I presume it is the experience of every author, after his first book is published upon an important subject, to be almost overwhelmed with a wealth of ideas and illustrations which could readily have been included in his book, and which to his own mind, at least, seem to make a second edition inevitable. Such certainly was the case with me; and when the first edition had reached its sixth impression in five months, I rejoiced to learn that it seemed to my publishers that the book had met with a sufficiently favorable reception to justify a second and considerably enlarged edition. ..

Pages:412

Reference   ISBN: *1-59462-647-2*   *MSRP $19.95*

On the Duty of Civil Disobedience
Henry David Thoreau

QTY

Thoreau wrote his famous essay, On the Duty of Civil Disobedience, as a protest against an unjust but popular war and the immoral but popular institution of slave-owning. He did more than write—he declined to pay his taxes, and was hauled off to gaol in consequence. Who can say how much this refusal of his hastened the end of the war and of slavery ?

Law   ISBN: *1-59462-747-9*   **Pages:48**

MSRP $7.45

Dream Psychology
Psychoanalysis for Beginners

Sigmund Freud

Dream Psychology Psychoanalysis for Beginners
Sigmund Freud

QTY

Sigmund Freud, born Sigismund Schlomo Freud (May 6, 1856 - September 23, 1939), was a Jewish-Austrian neurologist and psychiatrist who co-founded the psychoanalytic school of psychology. Freud is best known for his theories of the unconscious mind, especially involving the mechanism of repression; his redefinition of sexual desire as mobile and directed towards a wide variety of objects; and his therapeutic techniques, especially his understanding of transference in the therapeutic relationship and the presumed value of dreams as sources of insight into unconscious desires.

Pages:196

Psychology   ISBN: *1-59462-905-6*   *MSRP $15.45*

The Miracle of Right Thought
Orison Swett Marden

QTY

Believe with all of your heart that you will do what you were made to do. When the mind has once formed the habit of holding cheerful, happy, prosperous pictures, it will not be easy to form the opposite habit. It does not matter how improbable or how far away this realization may see, or how dark the prospects may be, if we visualize them as best we can, as vividly as possible, hold tenaciously to them and vigorously struggle to attain them, they will gradually become actualized, realized in the life. But a desire, a longing without endeavor, a yearning abandoned or held indifferently will vanish without realization.

Pages:360

Self Help   ISBN: *1-59462-644-8*   *MSRP $25.45*

QTY

The Rosicrucian Cosmo-Conception Mystic Christianity *by Max Heindel*   ISBN: *1-59462-188-8*   **$38.95**
The Rosicrucian Cosmo-conception is not dogmatic, neither does it appeal to any other authority than the reason of the student. It is: not controversial, but is: sent forth in the, hope that it may help to clear...   New Age/Religion Pages 646

Abandonment To Divine Providence *by Jean-Pierre de Caussade*   ISBN: *1-59462-228-0*   **$25.95**
"The Rev. Jean Pierre de Caussade was one of the most remarkable spiritual writers of the Society of Jesus in France in the 18th Century. His death took place at Toulouse in 1751. His works have gone through many editions and have been republished...   Inspirational/Religion Pages 400

Mental Chemistry *by Charles Haanel*   ISBN: *1-59462-192-6*   **$23.95**
Mental Chemistry allows the change of material conditions by combining and appropriately utilizing the power of the mind. Much like applied chemistry creates something new and unique out of careful combinations of chemicals the mastery of mental chemistry...   New Age Pages 354

The Letters of Robert Browning and Elizabeth Barret Barrett 1845-1846 vol II   ISBN: *1-59462-193-4*   **$35.95**
by Robert Browning and Elizabeth Barrett   Biographies Pages 596

Gleanings In Genesis (volume I) *by Arthur W. Pink*   ISBN: *1-59462-130-6*   **$27.45**
Appropriately has Genesis been termed "the seed plot of the Bible" for in it we have, in germ form, almost all of the great doctrines which are afterwards fully developed in the books of Scripture which follow...   Religion/Inspirational Pages 420

The Master Key *by L. W. de Laurence*   ISBN: *1-59462-001-6*   **$30.95**
In no branch of human knowledge has there been a more lively increase of the spirit of research during the past few years than in the study of Psychology, Concentration and Mental Discipline. The requests for authentic lessons in Thought Control, Mental Discipline and...   New Age/Business Pages 422

The Lesser Key Of Solomon Goetia *by L. W. de Laurence*   ISBN: *1-59462-092-X*   **$9.95**
This translation of the first book of the "Lernegton" which is now for the first time made accessible to students of Talismanic Magic was done, after careful collation and edition, from numerous Ancient Manuscripts in Hebrew, Latin, and French...   New Age/Occult Pages 92

Rubaiyat Of Omar Khayyam *by Edward Fitzgerald*   ISBN: *1-59462-332-5*   **$13.95**
Edward Fitzgerald, whom the world has already learned, in spite of his own efforts to remain within the shadow of anonymity, to look upon as one of the rarest poets of the century, was born at Bredfield, in Suffolk, on the 31st of March, 1809. He was the third son of John Purcell...   Music Pages 172

Ancient Law *by Henry Maine*   ISBN: *1-59462-128-4*   **$29.95**
The chief object of the following pages is to indicate some of the earliest ideas of mankind, as they are reflected in Ancient Law, and to point out the relation of those ideas to modern thought.   Religiom/History Pages 452

Far-Away Stories *by William J. Locke*   ISBN: *1-59462-129-2*   **$19.45**
"Good wine needs no bush, but a collection of mixed vintages does. And this book is just such a collection. Some of the stories I do not want to remain buried for ever in the museum files of dead magazine-numbers an author's not unpardonable vanity..."   Fiction Pages 272

Life of David Crockett *by David Crockett*   ISBN: *1-59462-250-7*   **$27.45**
"Colonel David Crockett was one of the most remarkable men of the times in which he lived. Born in humble life, but gifted with a strong will, an indomitable courage, and unremitting perseverance...   Biographies/New Age Pages 424

Lip-Reading *by Edward Nitchie*   ISBN: *1-59462-206-X*   **$25.95**
Edward B. Nitchie, founder of the New York School for the Hard of Hearing, now the Nitchie School of Lip-Reading, Inc, wrote "LIP-READING Principles and Practice". The development and perfecting of this meritorious work on lip-reading was an undertaking...   How-to Pages 400

A Handbook of Suggestive Therapeutics, Applied Hypnotism, Psychic Science   ISBN: *1-59462-214-0*   **$24.95**
by Henry Munro   Health/New Age/Health/Self-help Pages 376

A Doll's House: and Two Other Plays *by Henrik Ibsen*   ISBN: *1-59462-112-8*   **$19.95**
Henrik Ibsen created this classic when in revolutionary 1848 Rome. Introducing some striking concepts in playwriting for the realist genre, this play has been studied the world over.   Fiction/Classics/Plays 308

The Light of Asia *by sir Edwin Arnold*   ISBN: *1-59462-204-3*   **$13.95**
In this poetic masterpiece, Edwin Arnold describes the life and teachings of Buddha. The man who was to become known as Buddha to the world was born as Prince Gautama of India but he rejected the worldly riches and abandoned the reigns of power when...   Religion/History/Biographies Pages 170

The Complete Works of Guy de Maupassant *by Guy de Maupassant*   ISBN: *1-59462-157-8*   **$16.95**
"For days and days, nights and nights, I had dreamed of that first kiss which was to consecrate our engagement, and I knew not on what spot I should put my lips..."   Fiction/Classics Pages 240

The Art of Cross-Examination *by Francis L. Wellman*   ISBN: *1-59462-309-0*   **$26.95**
Written by a renowned trial lawyer, Wellman imparts his experience and uses case studies to explain how to use psychology to extract desired information through questioning.   How-to/Science/Reference Pages 408

Answered or Unanswered? *by Louisa Vaughan*   ISBN: *1-59462-248-5*   **$10.95**
Miracles of Faith in China   Religion Pages 112

The Edinburgh Lectures on Mental Science (1909) *by Thomas*   ISBN: *1-59462-008-3*   **$11.95**
This book contains the substance of a course of lectures recently given by the writer in the Queen Street Hall, Edinburgh. Its purpose is to indicate the Natural Principles governing the relation between Mental Action and Material Conditions...   New Age/Psychology Pages 148

Ayesha *by H. Rider Haggard*   ISBN: *1-59462-301-5*   **$24.95**
Verily and indeed it is the unexpected that happens! Probably if there was one person upon the earth from whom the Editor of this, and of a certain previous history, did not expect to hear again...   Classics Pages 380

Ayala's Angel *by Anthony Trollope*   ISBN: *1-59462-352-X*   **$29.95**
The two girls were both pretty, but Lucy who was twenty-one who supposed to be simple and comparatively unattractive, whereas Ayala was credited, as her Bombwhat romantic name might show, with poetic charm and a taste for romance. Ayala when her father died was nineteen...   Fiction Pages 484

The American Commonwealth *by James Bryce*   ISBN: *1-59462-286-8*   **$34.45**
An interpretation of American democratic political theory. It examines political mechanics and society from the perspective of Scotsman James Bryce   Politics Pages 572

Stories of the Pilgrims *by Margaret P. Pumphrey*   ISBN: *1-59462-116-0*   **$17.95**
This book explores pilgrims religious oppression in England as well as their escape to Holland and eventual crossing to America on the Mayflower, and their early days in New England...   History Pages 268

QTY

The Fasting Cure *by Sinclair Upton*   ISBN: *1-59462-222-1* **$13.95**
*In the Cosmopolitan Magazine for May, 1910, and in the Contemporary Review (London) for April, 1910, I published an article dealing with my experi-
ences in fasting. I have written a great many magazine articles, but never one which attracted so much attention... New Age/Self Help/Health Pages 164*

Hebrew Astrology *by Sepharial*   ISBN: *1-59462-308-2* **$13.45**
*In these days of advanced thinking it is a matter of common observation that we have left many of the old landmarks behind and that we are now pressing
forward to greater heights and to a wider horizon than that which represented the mind-content of our progenitors...   Astrology Pages 144*

Thought Vibration or The Law of Attraction in the Thought World   ISBN: *1-59462-127-6* **$12.95**

by William Walker Atkinson   *Psychology/Religion Pages 144*

Optimism *by Helen Keller*   ISBN: *1-59462-108-X* **$15.95**
*Helen Keller was blind, deaf, and mute since 19 months old, yet famously learned how to overcome these handicaps, communicate with the world, and
spread her lectures promoting optimism. An inspiring read for everyone...   Biographies/Inspirational Pages 84*

Sara Crewe *by Frances Burnett*   ISBN: *1-59462-360-0* **$9.45**
*In the first place, Miss Minchin lived in London. Her home was a large, dull, tall one, in a large, dull square, where all the houses were alike, and all the
sparrows were alike, and where all the door-knockers made the same heavy sound...   Childrens/Classic Pages 88*

The Autobiography of Benjamin Franklin *by Benjamin Franklin*   ISBN: *1-59462-135-7* **$24.95**
*The Autobiography of Benjamin Franklin has probably been more extensively read than any other American historical work, and no other book of its kind
has had such ups and downs of fortune. Franklin lived for many years in England, where he was agent...   Biographies/History Pages 332*

Name	
Email	
Telephone	
Address	
City, State ZIP	

☐ **Credit Card**   ☐ **Check / Money Order**

Credit Card Number	
Expiration Date	
Signature	

Please Mail to: Book Jungle
PO Box 2226
Champaign, IL 61825
or Fax to: 630-214-0564

ORDERING INFORMATION

web: *www.bookjungle.com*
email: *sales@bookjungle.com*
fax: *630-214-0564*
mail: *Book Jungle PO Box 2226 Champaign, IL 61825*
or PayPal *to sales@bookjungle.com*

Please contact us for bulk discounts

DIRECT-ORDER TERMS

**20% Discount if You Order
Two or More Books**
Free Domestic Shipping!
Accepted: Master Card, Visa,
Discover, American Express

www.ingramcontent.com/pod-product-compliance
Lightning Source LLC
Chambersburg PA
CBHW080824020726
47501CB00009B/2411